A
FAIRBANKS
AFFAIR

An Odds-Are-Good Standalone Romance

New York Times Bestselling Author
KATY REGNERY

Please visit my website at **www.katyregnery.com**
Cover Designer: Marianne Nowicki
Developmental Edit: Tessa Shapcott
Formatting: CookieLynn Publishing Services

First Edition: December 2019
A Fairbanks Affair: a novel / by Katy Regnery—1st ed.
ISBN: 978-1-944810-56-6

For Autumn and Tree.
I love you two.
xoxo

And for the lady at Ka-Fo,
who said I could stay.

CHAPTER ONE

Faye

A FAIRBANKS AFFAIR
Tall, dark, and single. 31.
Clean, safe, and solvent.
Seeking a discreet holiday companion
for an intimate New Year's weekend.
Three nights. Two of us. One hotel room.
Zero chance of love.
All expenses paid for the chosen candidate.
Please include photo with reply.

It's not that I look at the ad *intentionally*.

No, no.

Absolutely not.

I am *not* the type of woman who skims the personals.

Here is what happens:

When I sit down in the waiting area of Dr. Lafferty's office, a magazine is open on the loveseat beside me, and the word "Fairbanks" catches my eye. And only then, I'm sure, because my company is trying to buy North Star Spirits, the premiere distillery of northern Alaska, which is located in Fairbanks.

When I realize that I'm looking at a personal ad, I snap

my eyes up and forward, focusing on a poster about Invisalign.

But while the minutes drag on, I find my eyes drawn back down to the words "A FAIRBANKS AFFAIR," and eventually curiosity gets the better of me.

Tall, dark, single. Thirty-one.

I purse my lips and roll my eyes.

Of course he is.

Though I must admit, I appreciate that he swaps out the usual "handsome" for "single." I certainly *hope* he's single, seeing as how this is a personal ad, but I would think it presumptuous if he declared himself handsome. Also noteworthy? At thirty-one, he's just a year older than me, which means I'm not the only person on the face of the planet about to spend the holidays alone.

Clean, safe, and solvent.

Interesting choice of words and information.

By "clean" and "safe," I assume he means to share that he's free of disease and won't physically harm the applicants, which is always a good thing when seeking a love interest.

And "solvent" means, well…that he has money. Enough of it to be comfortable. *Good for you*, I think, giving him extra points for the correct use of an unusual word.

Seeking a discreet holiday companion…

Discreet.

Why? I wonder.

If he's single, why does he require secrecy? Or maybe he means that he's seeking someone mature and tactful? Or maybe—*my imagination is running away with me a little now!*—he's famous and doesn't want to draw unwanted attention? It's a mystery.

My eyes slip back to the text…

…for an intimate New Year's Weekend.

Intimate. I blink at the word. *Oh my.* It's just so…*bold.* So brash and confident and yes, a little cheeky too. He's placed this personal ad to find someone—a stranger—willing to be intimate with him for a weekend. He's essentially seeking an anonymous sex partner, right? My skin prickles. Why wouldn't he pay for such services if he requires them? Wouldn't that be easier? *But maybe,* I think, my inner voice breathless, *not as much fun.*

Three nights. Two of us. One hotel room.

Well, if the previous line didn't spell out his intentions, this one certainly does.

My cheeks flare with heat, and I clear my throat, glancing around the dentist's office waiting room like I've been caught doing something naughty, which a laugh, because I haven't done something naughty in…in…Lord, I can't actually remember the last time I threw caution to the wind! And certainly I can't remember a time I've ever spent three nights in a hotel room with a strange single man. *Likely because you've never found yourself in a situation even remotely similar, Faye.* The simple fact is this: I've never spent a night with any man, anywhere, at any time.

Zero chance of love.

"But *why?*"

The whispered words escape my lips in a rush, without permission.

3

"Excuse me?" I look up to find the receptionist eyeing me, one eyebrow raised. "Did you say something?"

"Oh!" I say with a soft, self-conscious chuckle. "I'm just…no, nothing. I was just…reading."

She smiles back. "It'll only be another minute or two, Ms. Findley. Sorry for the wait."

"No worries."

I wait until she's concentrating on her computer screen again, then slide my eyes back to the ad, staring at the words *"Zero chance of love"* for a long moment, fascinated that he's so forthcoming and so final. How can he *know* there's zero chance of love? Because he doesn't want it? Or because he's immune to it? Maybe he thinks he's not worthy of it? Or perhaps he's just monumentally busy and doesn't have time—at this point in his life—to nurture attraction into love?

For reasons I cannot begin to explain, it makes me terribly sad.

I certainly haven't had much luck with love over my three decades on earth, but that doesn't mean I don't want it. I'd like to think there's still a chance for me to find love, even if it isn't an epic, heart-pounding, life-changing love. At this point, I think I could be happy with someone kind and understanding, who wanted to build a partnership together. Maybe even someone who could be happy with gender roles reversed; I would happily make the money if he would do the shopping and make dinner, take care of our home, and plan social events for us to attend. Doesn't someone like that exist? He's got to be out there—someone bright and sweet: a good, strong man who isn't intimidated by a successful woman.

"Ms. Findley? Dr. Lafferty will see you now," announces the receptionist. "Exam room four, please."

"Oh!" I chirp, startled out of my runaway thoughts. "Yes. Thank you."

I stand up then freeze, glancing back down at the ad and feeling a connection to it, however surprising and unlikely. It's not for *me* to answer it, of course, but I can't help but wonder if Mr. Fairbanks will find a discreet woman to be his New Year's companion and, if so, how she will comply with his ultimatum about love.

"Ms. Findley? They're ready."

"Yes! Sorry."

I start walking toward the door that leads back to Dr. Lafferty's exam rooms, then turn around and hurry back to the loveseat. Without thinking, I snatch up the magazine and jam it into the murky depths of my enormous purse, then continue on to exam room four.

"Good morning, Ms. Findley," greets a chipper dental hygienist.

"Hello," I say, holding my purse close like I've shoved a rare Ming vase into it and don't want to be caught red-handed.

"You can put your bag on the chair," she says. "Dr. Lafferty will be with you in a moment to numb things up, and then we'll get started."

"How long will this take?" I ask, zipping the top of my purse closed before taking a seat in the dental chair.

"Looks like we have…two cavities? Hmm. Well, ten to fifteen minutes for the Novocain. Thirty minutes for each filling. Then a little filing. Maybe ninety minutes all together?"

"I have an important meeting at one," I tell her as she clips a bib around my neck.

"That shouldn't be a problem," she tells me.

Cheerful Christmas music is piped into the room, and "Santa Claus Is Coming to Town" starts as Dr. Lafferty enters the room.

"Faye! Good to see you!"

Is it me, or do dentists try too hard to be cheerful? I really don't want to be here, and we both know it. Cut it out with the holly jolly hello, and let's get on with the stabbing and drilling.

"Happy holidays, Dr. Lafferty."

"And to you!" He opens a file. "Two cavities today, eh?"

"I guess so."

"Let's see what's going on here." As I lean back and open wide, he rubs a Q-tip on my gums. "We'll give that a second. It's a topical anesthetic." He smiles at me. "So…what's new? Any big holiday plans?"

"Not really," I say.

"Harry's coming home, right?"

He's referring to my younger sister, Harriet, who is ten years my junior and also his patient. Harry's a junior at Cornell University in Upstate New York, about a six-hour drive from where I live in Newton, Massachusetts, a suburb of Boston. Not that it really matters where she goes to school or where I live, because she won't be in either place for Christmas or New Year's.

"Um. No," I say. "Actually, she was invited to Vail with a friend for winter break. So she'll be heading out to Colorado on Friday."

"But surely…" he begins, then closes his mouth and gives me a sad smile. "I guess I just assumed you ladies would spend the holidays together."

"Not this year," I say softly.

My feelings were a little hurt when Harriet chose friends over me for Christmas and New Year's, but I can't blame her. The reality is that she'll have a much better time with her friends. As she pointed out, last Christmas, we slept in, opened presents, and had lunch at my country club, after which I went up to my study to work while she hung out alone in the TV room watching Christmas movies. I'm sorry it ended up that way, but one of our major champagne suppliers had a transportation issue that could have precluded them from getting a massive shipment to California in time for New Year's. I needed to iron it out or risk the reputation of my family's company. I just wish Harry could have tried harder to understand.

"I remember the last Christmas your parents were alive," he says, his voice gentle. "They were great people, Dave and Margaret."

"Thank you," I whisper, swallowing over a small lump in my throat. Their memory is bittersweet.

My parents died eight years ago when their private

plane hit stormy weather between Nantucket and Manhattan, leaving me—just twenty-two at the time—the guardian and caregiver of my twelve-year-old sister. Because I was in grad school and didn't feel I had the luxury of dropping out to be a full-time parent—especially since the future of Findley Imports rested on my young shoulders—I enrolled Harriet at Deerfield Academy, from which both my father and I matriculated.

"I guess you're ready for that shot now," says Dr. Lafferty. I open my mouth, and he sticks his gloved hands inside to give me the Novocain injection. "So how *will* you spend Christmas this year, Faye?"

"Uhhhh." I wince at the weird sensation of Novocain spreading out along my gums. "I a-n't de-ci d yeh."

"Haven't decided yet, eh?"

It's remarkable to me that dentists understand garbling so well. It really is a skill.

"Well, I guess you've still got a week or so to figure it out." He rubs my gums to spread the analgesic. "I watched a great show on the Travel Channel recently…all about Christmas festivals around the world. There's one in Hyde Park I'd love to see sometime."

"Im Lon-non o-ah New Yor?"

"London. And of course in Germany, they've got a Christkindlmarkt in just about every city. I didn't know, but Budapest has an enormous festival, as well." He gestures to his assistant. "She's ready. Let's get started."

I stare up at the bright light over the dental chair as various instruments slide in and out of my mouth. A

Christmas festival. Hmm. That's not such a bad idea.

Our offices are closed from December 24 to 26 and again from December 31 to January 2, and I haven't taken a vacation in four years. While Harry's and my Christmases aren't super exciting, I always looked forward to having her home for a week. Being alone in my big, old house over Christmas and New Year's sounds like Miss Havisham–levels of depressing.

"In Finland, there's a place called Santa Claus Village," Dr. Lafferty continues. "Beautiful spot."

"Im app-ann?"

"Uh-huh. In Lapland," he answers, the whirr of the drill strangely soothing when it isn't accompanied by pain. "That looked pretty cool. Ha ha. Literally. Snowy Nordic weather, you know? Moose. Reindeer."

I close my eyes as he drills and fills, thinking about the last time I was in Finland, just a few months ago. It was to visit distilleries, however, not Santa Claus.

I've spent a good deal of time in Scandinavia, where some of the best vodkas in the world are made. I like Copenhagen and Stockholm especially, and I briefly consider the option of spending Christmas in either, though the thought leaves me feeling figuratively—well, and literally, I guess—cold. I don't speak Danish or Swedish very well, and all my contacts in both cities are business-related, not personal friends who might include me in their holiday celebrations.

"Speaking of cold places, did you know there's a town in Alaska called North Pole? Yep. Adorable. They do a whole festival there called 'Christmas in Ice.' The northern lights. Santa's house. Ha ha. Cute for the kids, I guess."

He packs some composite on the now-cleaned cavity, then uses an ultraviolet light to harden the polymer while I sit back and think about this.

No, I didn't know there was a place in Alaska called North Pole, but I'm unaccountably intrigued.

"Oo oo oh whe-ah it is?"

"North Pole, Alaska? Yes, I do. About twenty minutes south of Fairbanks." Again, Dr. Lafferty has mad skills with the garbling. It's uncanny.

Twenty minutes south of…Fairbanks.

Hmm. Is it just me, or do all roads point to Fairbanks today?

Fairbanks, of North Star Distillery and North Pole fame, is also the home of a certain bachelor seeking holiday companionship.

How about Christmas in the North Pole and New Year's in Fairbanks?

The question slides through my mind like the slow-motion replay of a puck sliding across the ice, and I watch the letters appear one after the other, until the question is crystal clear and lingers, like the light of a camera flash, in my mind.

As Dr. Lafferty preps the second cavity for filling, the following internal conversation ensues:

No. I couldn't.

Why not?

Because…I'm not that sort of woman.

The sort who has sex with strangers?

The sort who has sex with…anyone.

But perhaps, my insistent mind continues, *this could be a chance to remedy that.*

Virginity is not a disease, I fire back. *It doesn't require a goddamned remedy!*

My mind lets the dust settle before asking,

Are you sure about that?

"How does that feel?" asks Dr. Lafferty. "Any pain?"

I've been so consumed with my thoughts, I've ignored everything else going on around me, but now I snap out of it.

"None," I manage through numbed lips.

"Terrific," he answers. "I'm just going to do a little smoothing and you'll be good to go."

"Perfect."

"The next time you come in," says Dr. Lafferty with a warm smile, "you'll have to let me know what you decided to do."

"To *do*?" I ask, horrified that he's somehow overheard my conversation with myself.

"For the holidays," he says. "And when you talk to her, please give Harry my very best."

***

"Dr. Lafferty sends his best."

"Who? The dentist?"

"Yes."

"Um…great. I guess."

I'm sitting on the loveseat in my bedroom, talking to

my little sister on the phone, a glass of very good red wine in my other hand. Chatting with Harriet has always been a struggle for me—never organic like with sisters in movies or on TV, who never have enough time to say everything and can't wait to catch up with one another.

Our parents had only intended to have one child: me. When my mother discovered she was pregnant with Harriet at forty-six years old, it was a tremendous shock, though one my parents received with gratitude and instant love.

At first, I resented my little sister, annoyed to have to share my parents after having them all to myself for so long. But honestly, the age difference, a full decade, was so significant, I needn't have worried. In a weird way, we were both like only children. Sibling rivalry was almost impossible.

On the day I got my driver's license, Harriet lost her first tooth.

When I graduated from undergrad, she was just finishing grade school.

And when our parents passed away, I was too busy with school and dealing with my own terrible grief to help her with hers.

When she was between the ages of twelve and eighteen, I made sure she had annual doctor and dentist appointments, wonderful summer camp experiences, and capable babysitters to be her companions whenever she was home for longer stretches. But are we close? No. We're not. We never have been.

"You've got your ticket for Vail?" I ask her.

"Mm-hm. Carlene e-mailed it to me."

Carlene is my assistant, and I've overheard them on the phone together more than once. I'm fairly certain that she and Harry are more like sisters than Harriet and I will ever be.

"First class?"

"I didn't check, but...oh yes. Thanks, Faye."

"Of course. I sent your gifts to the address you gave me," I tell her. "And I included a host gift, as well. It's a Tiffany vase. Please see that your friend's mother receives it."

"Sure." She pauses for a second. "Are you—I mean, do you have plans? What are you going to do for Christmas?"

Across the room I spy my purse, sitting on the desk in my bedroom where I opened my laptop a few hours ago. "I may travel a bit."

"Oh! Oh, that's great, Faye."

There's relief in my little sister's voice, and it surprises me a little.

"Were you worried about me, Harriet?"

"Not really. You're so...independent. I just—well, I'm glad you're going somewhere, doing something. To celebrate. It's good. Where are you headed?"

"We're trying to acquire a distillery in Alaska," I say. "I may go have a peek at it."

Her tone dips drastically. "Oh."

"What?"

"You're working."

"A little, yes."

"I thought—I mean, I *hoped*—you were doing

13

something just for you."

"I *am* doing something just for me."

"Actually, it sounds like you're traveling for Findley Imports."

"Is that a bad thing?"

My sister pauses for a second before speaking. "Not bad, per se. But it's your whole life. It *has* been, ever since Mommy and Daddy passed away."

"I think our father would have wanted it that way," I tell her. "I could have shirked my responsibility, I suppose, but think of how disappointed he would have been. He and Grandpa built Findley Imports from the ground up. The least I could do is—"

"Fine, Faye! You win. You win."

I furrow my eyebrows. "Is this a win-or-lose situation?"

"No. It's just—forget it," she says. "I hope you have a nice time wherever you're going."

"Me too."

"You said Alaska, right? Where? Anchorage?"

"Fairbanks area," I say, taking another sip of wine and reminding myself to speak to Carlene about having our acquisitions department reach out to this vineyard. It's damn good. We should be selling it.

"You seem busy," says Harriet. "I'll let you go."

"Right. I'll call on Christmas…Not to bother you. Just for a quick hello."

"It doesn't bother me when you call," she says, her voice soft and frustrated.

"Well, I wouldn't want to interfere with your plans," I

tell her. Something inside me pinches a little, but I don't know why, and I'm really not interested in rooting around in my psyche to create a problem where there is none. I make sure my voice is crisp and upbeat when I add, "Be a good houseguest."

"I will."

"And safe travels."

"You too, Faye," she says. "Merry Christmas."

"Yes, of course. Merry Christmas, Harriet," I finish, lowering the phone from my ear and hanging up.

I place the phone on the arm of the loveseat, staring at it for a second as I realize how quiet the house is.

I live in a Greek Revival mansion, built in the 1870s, when Newton became one of the first bustling suburbs of Boston. Two years after my parents died, I finally decided I'd had enough of apartment living, and when this house, located on Valentine Street and sporting original murals in the upstairs hallway, became available, I snatched it up right away. But with three floors, five bedrooms, and six thousand square feet of space, it's a ridiculous size for a single woman.

I should sell it, I think.

But where would I go then? Back to the city? Ugh. No. Maybe just to a smaller house in Newton, with just enough space for me and Harriet, on the occasional weekend that she wants to come and visit.

A dreadful melancholy washes over me as I consider the prospect of downsizing.

I don't know that I ever thought of getting married and raising children in this house, but maybe I did—somewhere in the back of my mind—when I purchased it. I was naïve at the time, however, and didn't realize the sheer number of hours it would take to keep my father's company alive and thriving. Well…that, and I quickly learned that men are intimidated by powerful, successful women. My dating life since taking over Findley Imports as CEO and president has been…negligible.

Again, my eyes land on my purse, and I cross the large bedroom to open the bag and pull out the magazine I stole from Dr. Lafferty's office this morning. Opening it properly, I learn from the cover that publication is called *The Odds Are Good*, and the tagline reads, *"The goods are odd, but the odds are good!"* Indeed.

Flipping through it as I finish my glass of cabernet, I quickly gather that this is a publication for Alaskan men seeking all manner of company from women in the Lower Forty-Eight. There are ads seeking girlfriends, sex partners, boyfriends, and even wives. I read a three-page story about a salmon fisherman in Ketchikan who's ready to settle down, and a two-page spread about a state trooper in Sitka who successfully found love via an *Odds Are Good* ad.

Finally, I flip to the end, where smaller ads are arranged in Personals and Classifieds, and my eyes are immediately drawn to Mr. Fairbanks' short and neat proposition.

My cheeks flush as I consider writing back to him, but I already know I'm going to. I have the same fluttering in my stomach that I sometimes get before I make a huge acquisition or substantial investment. Excitement. Fear. The thrill of making a brash decision that could pay off big. It's just that I generally make such bold moves in business, not in my personal life.

Not that I won't, like any good businesswoman, take some steps to mitigate my risk:

First, I don't plan to use my real name. I'll use a variation on my first name—Faith, instead of Faye—and my mother's maiden name, Crawford, as a surname. Since Crawford is also my middle name, it isn't really lying, right? Right.

Second, If I'm chosen, I will insist on seeing actual medical records to back up Mr. Fairbanks' claims of being "clean," and I will offer to send the same to him, not that he need worry.

And third, I do not require any remuneration for my travels, though he's welcome to pay for our hotel room if it pleases him.

My feelings about my virginity are...complicated, but I'll not allow them to shanghai this experience away from me. I'll answer the ad tonight and deal with them between now and meeting Mr. Fairbanks. After all, I might not even be chosen.

Luckily, I have just the right picture to send. It was taken by Harriet last summer while we were sailing off the coast of Nantucket. I'm tall and tan, with my rosewood-colored hair unbound, the dark tresses flying back in the breeze as the sun picks out the natural red highlights. Because my sailing clothes had gotten soaked, necessitating a change I'd forgotten to bring, I'd borrowed an outfit from Harry: I'm wearing my white oversized Chanel sunglasses, with Harriet's white bikini top and cutoff denim shorts.

On a regular day, I look nothing like the girl in the photo whatsoever.

But it is my favorite picture of myself.

I keep it in my desk, and sometimes I take it out and look at it, knowing it's me and yet marveling at how completely different I appear: young and fun and carefree. And sometimes, when I'm being completely honest, I'll admit to myself that the girl in the photo looks like someone I *wish* I could be.

I pull my laptop from the coffee table in front of me, trading it for my empty wineglass, and settle the computer on my lap as it boots up. Then I open the internet, click on my e-mail program, enter in the address accompanying Mr. Fairbanks' ad, and begin typing.

CHAPTER TWO

Trevor

Of all the responses I received to my ad—and there were over a hundred—there is one that captures my attention more than any of the others.

It arrived yesterday, later than the rest, and the woman who wrote it used careful, grammatically perfect English, giving a thoughtful response to my ad without being crude or tawdry. Bearing in mind that most of the other responses eschewed tasteful euphemisms for "dirty" language—*perhaps the frankness of my proposition led them to believe I would embrace such vulgarity?*—hers stands out among them.

I stare at the picture of the girl on the boat for the twentieth time today.

There's something about her, standing on the front deck of a sailboat with the wind blowing through her hair. I can't tell where the picture was taken, but it doesn't matter. I just wish I was standing beside her.

My brother Baz walks into my office at North Star Spirits. "Did we decide on the label for the vanilla-infused vodka?"

"Not yet."

He holds up two differently designed vodka bottles. "Vanilla bean or ice cream cone?"

I glance up. "Neither. I hate them both."

"Want me to try whipped cream?"

"Yuck. It'll look cheap, Baz. Our product is high end. Classy."

"Then we go with the vanilla bean. Stoli, Skyy, and Smirnoff do the bean on their vanilla bottles."

"Then it's being overdone."

"A thousand problems and not one solution," my brother gripes.

It was my grandfather's favorite catchphrase when someone had a lot of complaints but no suggestions for making things better.

"Just…give me a second." I close my eyes and think of vanilla…sweet, festive, a little bit sexy. I open my eyes and snap my fingers. "How about…cream-colored silk?"

"Like a ribbon?"

"Or a scarf. Yeah. Circling the bottle."

"Could work," says Baz. "And I don't think anyone else is doing it."

"There we go. My work here is done," I say, sliding my eyes back to Faith Crawford.

"What have you been doing in here all morning?" asks Baz, circling my desk before I can minimize the photo. "Whoa. Who's that?"

"Faith Crawford."

"How do you know her?"

"I don't," I say too quickly. Shoot! I do not need for my brother to know that I placed a personal ad for female companionship. He'd never let me live it down. "The, uh, the PR company in San Francisco sent over some headshots for a possible spokesperson."

"Hmm. Well…I get the appeal, but I don't think she works. She's too young and flirty," says Baz. "We need someone with more gravitas. Weren't we leaning toward the middle-aged man concept they pitched us?"

"Yeah," I say.

He's correct—Faith Crawford is young, flirty, and utterly mouth-watering but is not right for our upcoming campaign whatsoever.

"She's pretty," he adds.

Actually, she's not pretty. She's *beautiful*. One of the most beautiful, effortlessly classy women I've ever seen.

Baz leans closer. "But she looks *really* expensive."

"What does that mean?" I ask, though his answer is irrelevant. I don't care if she's "expensive." She's the woman with whom I want to spend New Year's weekend.

He flicks his fingers at the screen. "Chanel sunglasses. And unless I'm mistaken, which I'm not, that watch is a Longines with a diamond bezel. If Chanel or Longines is paying her to do their ads, she's probably out of our budget, bro."

"How do you have room in your brain for all that random shit?" I demand.

He shrugs. My little brother's photographic memory means that he is full of extraneous information.

"Then again," Baz continues, "if you want to go in a different direction, and go for a more sexy campaign, Cez and I won't stand in your way."

I own fifty-one percent of North Star Spirits, but the other forty-nine percent of my company is split between my twin brothers, Basil, whom we call "Baz," and Cecil, whom we call "Cez," pronounced like "cease." They each have an almost one-quarter share in the company I started.

"Speaking of the devil's spawn, how's he doing?" I ask, minimizing Faith Crawford's photo and moving on to less pleasant matters.

"If he's the devil's spawn, then we are too. We were all *spawned* in the same place," says Baz, stepping away from my desk to sit in one of the guest chairs across from me. I stare at Baz until he squirms and says, "I'm not on his side, Trev."

"Are you on *mine*?"

"What Cez did was wrong, but—"

"But *he's* your twin. *I'm* just your brother."

"You're *both* my brothers!" Baz's face registers frustration before he looks away from me, taking a deep breath and sighing. "Wasn't it—at least partially—Marlena's fault too?"

I nod. "Yep. Sure was."

"But Cez is the one you banished."

"I didn't *banish* him, Johnny-drama."

"You broke two of his ribs, said that you weren't brothers anymore, and told him never to show his face in Fairbanks again as long as you lived."

"I said never to show his face in my *distillery* again."

"Same difference."

"Baz! He slept with my fiancée—"

"I know."

"—on the night before my wedding—"

"I know."

"—*and* got her *pregnant!*"

"I know!" yells Baz, clenching his jaw before looking away from me. "It sucks."

"*Cez* sucks," I say. "He is—*was*—my brother! He should have kept his hands off what was mine!"

"'*What was mine*'? Do you hear yourself? What woman wants to be with a man who thinks of her as his property, Trev?"

My eyes pop out of my head. "Oh, so this is *my* fault?"

"Maybe. Some of it. Are you sure you and Marlena had the healthiest relationship?"

"I don't know, Baz. All I know is that I didn't fuck my brother's fiancée."

Baz's shoulders slump as he sighs.

"Cez was my brother…my flesh and blood!"

I blink at Baz, my chest aching and eyes burning. It's been over six months, but discussing Cecil's betrayal still cuts deep and hurts really fucking bad.

"So is the baby she's carrying," says Baz softly. "He or she is your flesh and blood too."

I inhale sharply. I don't know if I'll ever be ready for a conversation about Cez and Marlena's child. I can barely talk about what my brother and fiancée did, let alone the result. I exhale slowly and flick a glance at the two bottles Baz deposited on the corner of my desk.

"I want to see a mock-up of the opaque bottle with the cream silk. When can you have it ready?"

Baz leans forward. "Trevor. Can we please talk about this?"

"Why?"

"Because…I know you hate him right now, and I know he *deserves* your anger. He betrayed you. It's true. There's no way around it. But Trev, he's our *brother*. He's sorry. He wants to talk."

I stare at Baz with dead eyes. "No."

"Come on. It's almost Christmas. You haven't seen him since June."

"I don't give a shit."

Baz purses his lips, then says, "I promised I wouldn't say anything, but…Mom and Dad invited Cez and Marlena to stop by on Christmas Eve."

My mouth drops open. "What the *fuck*? They *invited* him?"

He shrugs. "Marlena's carrying their grandchild, Trev."

I can't handle this. My head's going to explode.

"Well, then you can tell Mom and Dad *I* won't be there for Christmas Eve."

"Come on," says Baz, sighing long and hard. "Mom's going to kill me for telling you."

"Luckily, you're her favorite," I say. "I'm sorry to get you into trouble, but thank you for letting me know."

"Reconsider, Trev. Just think about coming?"

"No," I say again, shuffling around some papers on my desk. "Get me that mock-up when you can, huh?"

My brother stands up, pushing the guest chair under the lip of my desk and taking his two bottles with him. When he gets to the door of my office, he turns around.

"He loves you, Trev."

"Fuck him."

"He does. He loves you."

"He has a funny way of showing it."

"You can't hate him forever."

"Maybe not," I say softly, "but I can't ever trust him again either."

Baz winces, then nods like he understands, pulling the door shut behind him as he leaves.

I spin around in my chair, looking through a large plate-glass window over the North Star Tasting Room, where we welcome visitors to try our various vodkas. Right now, there are four women clustered on one side of the bar and a couple sitting side by side on two barstools. I stare at the couple for a second, remembering not so long ago when I was half of a couple too.

Marlena Hopkins and I met in the emergency room of Fairbanks Memorial Hospital three years ago, when I came in with a dislocated shoulder and she was one of the nurses on duty. With blonde curls and bright-blue eyes, set off by the ice-blue color of her scrubs, I was smitten before the doctor even came in, and I had her number in my pocket before I left.

Twenty-two to my twenty-seven, Marlena was bubbly, sweet, and young. Though she'd grown up in Portland and graduated from the University of Oregon, she'd taken a job in Fairbanks because she thought Alaska would be exciting.

"Maybe I was hoping to meet a rich gold miner," she'd

joked on one of our first dates.

"Would you settle for a distiller instead?"

"Are you gonna be rich?" she'd asked, her pretty eyes bright and sparkling.

"Yes," I'd promised her. "If that's what you want."

At the time, I was in the process of building our first distillery. Having grown up on the largest potato farm in the state of Alaska, I'd always had a notion of expanding the family business to include spirits. I just had no idea how widely and warmly our vodka would be received, first in Alaska and then in the Lower Forty-Eight as well.

Am I rich? Turning around in my chair, I nod my head before leaning back with a sigh. *Yes, I am.*

On my desk is a picture of the home I built last year: six thousand square feet on ten acres. It's got five bedrooms, four bathrooms, a full deck and patio, and a top-of-the-line kitchen with every cutting-edge toy and convenience. It has four fireplaces—one each in the great room, sitting room, master bedroom, and my office—and a three-car garage. There's a sauna and hot tub inside, with massive windows for watching the northern lights, and a game room in the basement with a TV so big that it practically takes up a full wall. Anywhere on earth it would be a showplace, and I built it for her…all for her.

Marlena.

I clench my jaw and rub my chin, remembering the night before my wedding. The rehearsal dinner at a Portland hotel had ended, but my future bride was nowhere to be found. I asked her friends if they'd seen her and even swung by her parent's house to see if she'd decided to spend the night before our wedding at home. Unable to find her, I'd given up the search, assuming she was staying at the apartment of one of her sisters.

When I knocked on Cez and Baz's hotel room door, hoping to share one last toast with them before retiring to bed, I could hear voices in their room. I pressed my ear to the door and heard the distinct sound of moaning. Growling. The squeal of mattress springs. The *clap-clap-clap* of one body slapping into another.

And then there was the soundtrack, which wasn't even muffled through the wooden hotel door: *Ah-ah-ah…Ohmigod, ohmigod…more, Cez! More, baby! Keep going! I need you! I love you! Oh, Cez!*

At first, because the voice was so similar to Marlena's, my brain automatically assumed it was one of her sisters.

Wow, I thought. *Like big brothe…like little brother. You go, Cez.*

For a second there, I was rooting for him.

And then I turned to see Baz walking down the hall toward me. And the thing about Baz? His face can't keep a secret. It can't. It doesn't know how.

All the color drained from his cheeks as he approached me.

His easygoing smile disappeared.

His eyebrows knitted together over wide, worried eyes.

He walked faster but looked away—at the corridor walls, at the carpet—anywhere except at me.

My skin might have prickled a little, but I still didn't

suspect what was going on. I'd had a few drinks. I was getting married in a matter of hours.

"Baz!" I'd greeted him. "Drink with me!"

"TREVOR!" he'd shouted in way too loud of a voice.

"We need one more toast!"

Baz shot a concerned look at the door, from which all sound had suddenly disappeared. He cocked his head toward the elevator bank at the end of the hallway. "Let's go to your room."

"No way! We need Cez too." I'd banged on the door. "Cez, you done? Ha ha ha! Come out! Have a drink with us! Come on, bro. Come on—"

The door opened and my jaw dropped.

It wasn't Isabella or Camila Hopkins who opened the door.

No.

It was my blushing bride-to-be, Marlena, wearing barely there pajamas, a sheen of sweat on her forehead.

"Hey," I said, grinning at her. "What are you—"

"Trev," she whispered, staring up at me.

And *still* it didn't register. Almost like my mind wouldn't allow it to be true.

"What're you *doing* in there? I heard Cez getting busy with one of your sis...ters..."

Behind her, my brother suddenly appeared, shame etched into his face as he stood with his arms crossed over his chest, clad only in a pair of boxers.

That's when an icy chill slid down my spine. I flicked my eyes from Cez to Marlena, from Marlena to Cez.

"No. No, you didn't...oh, my God," I whispered.

"Trevor," said Cez, pushing past Marlena to get to me. "Wait!"

But I was already backing away, my stomach roiling and churning, my fists balling at my sides.

"Cez, go back inside!" cried Baz.

"No!" yelled Cez. "I have to explain! He deserves to understand!"

Fuck this. Fuck this. Fuck this. I was practically running toward the elevators, when I turned around and stalked back toward my brother.

"*Understand?*" I bellowed.

"Please, Trev. Please, let me—"

"WHAT. THE. FUCK?" I demanded. Out of the corner of my eye, I could see Marlena, still standing in the doorway of my brothers' hotel room, with tears sliding down her beautiful face. But it was Cecil—my baby brother, whom I loved, whom I had fucking *loved* since the day he was born—that I was looking at. "How could you fucking do this to me?"

Cez ran a hand through his thick dark hair and stood there in the hotel hallway in his underwear, shaking his head. "I didn't mean for it to happen, Trev."

"You didn't...mean to? FUCK YOU, CEZ! Your dick just happened to slide into my fiancée?"

His head twisted slightly to look at her, then he faced me again, but my fists had a mind of their own. I barreled into my brother, sitting on top of his chest and punching him relentlessly. His head. His face. His neck. His shoulders.

Everywhere. A flurry of forward motion and every word punctuated with the smash of my knuckles into his flesh.

"YOU. ARE. NOT. MY. BROTHER. ANY. MORE! I hate you! I hate you! Don't ever show your face near me again! I fucking hate you forever!"

Baz was trying to pull me off of Cez and told me later that Cez hadn't landed one punch, hadn't even tried to hit me back, had just laid there on the hotel carpeting, accepting my fury.

With two other hotel guests—some Hopkins cousins from Seattle woken up with the fracas—Baz was finally able to pull me off Cecil, who curled up into a bloody, battered ball. Marlena knelt beside him, eventually helping him to his feet and driving him to the hospital.

As for me?

Still fighting against the men holding me, I was somehow maneuvered into the elevator and then into my hotel room, where Baz poured so much vodka down my throat, I slept through the time when my wedding was scheduled to take place.

I found out later that Baz had knocked on every hotel room door, telling our guests that the wedding was off. Then sometime after noon, he returned to my hotel room, woke me up, waited as I vomited my guts out, drove me to the airport, and put me on a plane back to Fairbanks.

When I got back to my dream house, every trace of Marlena was already gone: her clothes, toiletries, throw pillows, decorations—all of them had been hastily removed by my parents, who'd arrived in Fairbanks several hours before me.

To this day, I haven't seen or spoken with Cez or Marlena.

But when Baz told me last month that Marlena was pregnant, I threw up into the garbage can under my desk before asking how far along she was. To my eternal confusion, I was both relieved and—how fucked up is this?—*disappointed* to realize that her baby couldn't possibly be mine.

The house in the picture is on the market now.

The only problem is that $1.2 million houses in Fairbanks, Alaska, don't sell too quickly. There just isn't a big market for them. So I live there—in the dream house I built to start a life with my brother's now-fiancée. And if that's not fucked up, I don't know what is.

Honestly, I think, reaching into the fridge under my desk for a bottle of beer and taking a nice, long sip, Marlena and Cez's betrayal has already had consequences I never could have imagined. I cannot think of a scenario in which I *ever* allow myself to fall in love again. Fuck love. Fuck loyalty. Fuck trust and honesty and forever.

They obviously weren't in the cards for me.

I make the best vodka in the state of Alaska, and it sells like it's the last batch I'll ever make. I'm rolling in dough.

Let that be enough, I silently pray.

Because if you can't trust your own brother, you can't trust anyone. And if your fiancée isn't loyal enough to keep her twat to herself, fuck the idea of a fairytale forever.

Fairytales are for chumps and children, idiots and

dreamers.

And me? I'm none of those things.

Not anymore.

***

I pay a local woman, Inez Hernandez, to clean my house, do my laundry, pick up my dry cleaning, and make my meals. She comes over twice a week to stock my refrigerator with Tupperware containers that read "Monday Breakfast" or "Thursday Dinner," which means I get a home-cooked meal every morning and every night.

Tonight's meal is Mexican lasagna, which I've had before and like. I pop it in the microwave and head to my bedroom to change into shorts and a T-shirt. I'll get on the treadmill for an hour after dinner.

My conversation with Baz made me a moody fucker for the rest of the day, and so I didn't return any calls and basically limited my interactions to no one. Since Cez and Marlena's betrayal, I've sent our marketing advisor, Penny, home in tears more than once, much to Baz's consternation. I'm pretty sure he has a thing for her, though he moves at the speed of glacial crawl, so it's unlikely that anything will happen between them this century.

I change into workout clothes just in time to hear the *ding* of the microwave downstairs telling me my dinner's ready. I begin to eat, alone at the kitchen counter in my way-too-big kitchen, wishing that I had company, then narrowing my eyes at my own weakness.

I don't want to talk to someone—I don't want to get to know them or, God forbid, *care* about them. I don't want them to *mean* anything to me. I just…I miss having someone around. And God in heaven,

I miss sex.

I miss it so bad sometimes it actually fucking *hurts*.

I haven't had sex since two months before the-wedding-that-never-happened, because Marlena had read an article in the *Knot* that said wedding night sex was unbelievably awesome when you make yourself wait for it. Little did I know, that was just an excuse. If my suspicions are correct, she'd started fucking my brother in April: right around the time she'd dipped out on *our* sex life.

None of which changes the fact that I haven't had sex in eight long months. At first? I didn't want to. My libido tanked after what happened and pretty much stayed that way all summer. But as summer turned into autumn? I don't know. I'm thirty-one, male, and stupid. My dick started making its needs known. And yeah, I guess I could've booked an escort, but I'm a respected businessman, and paying for sex can get you in hot water. So if I didn't pay for it, I'd have to find a partner. And my mind had trouble figuring out how find someone when my heart refused to be a part of the act.

The bottom line is that I want it—I *need* it—to be on *my* terms. The very terms I laid out in my *The Odds Are Good* ad.

Anonymous. Short-term. With someone I'll never see again.

Someone like Faith Crawford.

Leaving my dinner for a second, I grab my laptop out of my bag and open it on the kitchen counter, taking a big bite of lasagna as it boots up.

I open my e-mail program and click on Faith's response to my ad.

I stare at her picture again while I finish eating my dinner on autopilot.

Unlike Marlena, she's a brunette, which instantly appealed to me. Also unlike Marlena, who had big tits and a very grabbable ass, she's lithe. She's about five foot eight and probably weighs a buck thirty. She's willowy. Feminine. Young. And she's not stupid. Her message proved that she grasped the nuances of my ad and would accept my terms without asking for more. That meant more to me than anything else—that we were on the same page.

I scroll up to read her message:

Dear Mr. Fairbanks:

I understand that you are seeking a woman with whom to spend your New Year's holiday and that you seek a casual relationship of an intimate and discreet nature.

Like you, I am clean, safe, and solvent, so I do not require your financial assistance to convey me to Fairbanks, though I would like a companion with whom to ring in the new year. I find you an apt candidate.

Should you be interested in furthering our discourse, I would welcome a reply complete with the assurance of your good health by a medical professional and an address and time at which to meet you on January 29 in Fairbanks.

With kind regards,

Faith Crawford

It's not sexy, I think, grinning at the screen. *That's for damn sure.*

But that's partially what makes it so perfect—she proves her discretion in the language she uses and her understanding of my requirements in a manner better suited to the boardroom than the bedroom…which is great. Per my wishes, she's treating this entire arrangement like a business transaction, not the first chapter of a love story.

I'm physically attracted to the girl in the photo, and her message checks every box for me. Perhaps we'll even have some interesting, intelligent conversation during our time together. Though I have zero interest in love, I have nothing against pleasure, and what's better than a decent chat over dinner followed by a good fuck? Frankly, just reading her response has put me into a better mood than I ever could have imagined.

My decision is made.

Dear Miss Crawford, I type in response.

I would love to welcome you to Alaska…

CHAPTER THREE

Faye

All that jazz about how "adorable" North Pole, Alaska, is?

Lies.

I look out the taxi window at the drab, white-gray landscape off the highway, waiting for the big reveal. Surely a place called North Pole will have an abundance of Christmas charm, as per Dr. Lafferty's rhapsodizing, but it simply doesn't materialize. There's a sign alerting me that we've arrived in North Pole and advertising Santa's house "1/2 mile up on the right," but that's it.

As we turn off the highway and into a strip mall, I realize I'm here.

I've arrived.

This is it.

With the exception of some candy cane–striped lampposts, I've arrived in a very tiny American town that appears to consist of a strip mall and motel.

Dr. Lafferty is a first-rate liar.

That's all I can think as my taxi pulls under the modest porte cochere of the North Pole Inn and stops beside the front door. Well, *that*…and that my assistant, Carlene, must have had the laugh of her life when she booked this trip for me. Since she claimed I was booked at the "nicest place in North Pole," I now must consider that this establishment is the *only* place in North Pole. Little better than the motel-style lodgings that line most highways, this hotel is no "inn." It's small, generic, and unimpressive, set back behind a Safeway grocery store and a far cry from the sorts of charming places in which I'm used to staying.

That said, however, I left from Logan in Boston at five this morning, had an eight o'clock meeting in Manhattan, left from Newark at ten, and arrived in Fairbanks at six forty-five, after a short layover in Seattle. Bearing in mind the time change, I have been traveling for approximately twenty hours, and I'm exhausted.

Praying for clean sheets, I heft my laptop bag higher onto my shoulder and pull my large rolling suitcase into the annoyingly kitschy lobby, wondering what the hell I'm doing here.

"Welcome to the North Pole, where every day is Christmas!" exclaims the elf-dressed desk attendant as I approach. "Except for today. Today is *Christmas Eve!*"

"Yes, it is," I confirm, stopping in front of the counter that separates us.

"Merry Christmas Eve, weary traveler! I'm Elf Nikki!"

"Um…thank you."

"Checking in?"

"Yes, please."

"How about some hot cocoa?" asks Elf Nikki, reaching under the counter and pulling out a ceramic mug in the shape of Santa's hat.

"No, thank you."

Undeterred by my lack of enthusiasm, she puts the mug away and winks at me. "How long are you staying in Santa's favorite hotel?"

If her smile gets any wider, I think, *she might hurt herself.*

"Er, um…two nights? I believe?"

"Christmas Eve and Christmas night! Wow! How wonderful!"

Wonderful?

I give her a weak smile then glance over my shoulder at the lobby Christmas tree, which is so metallic and shiny, it makes me long for a pair of sunglasses. That it spins on a base and plays "Holly Jolly Christmas" in electronic tones isn't helping things.

"Oooo! You've booked one of our Santa Suites, Faye…*Kringle!*"

"My last name is Findley," I say, turning back to her.

"Not anymore! Everyone's a Kringle here!" Elf Nikki crows. "We're one big happy family in the North Pole."

"I see."

"Will you be joining us in the dining room for Christmas Eve dinner?"

My mouth waters, reminding me it's been a while since I last ate. "Yes. Thank you."

"We ask folks to prepay on busy nights. That'll be $12.95 for the buffet."

"What buffet?"

"The Christmas Eve dinner buffet," she says, still grinning at me.

For the first time, I wonder if she's not actually human but rather an automaton of some kind. Her smile hasn't dipped or wavered since I entered the room.

"Christmas Eve dinner is a…buffet?"

"Yes indeed! Baked ham, whipped potatoes, boiled green beans, chicken nuggets, fries, and mac 'n cheese. Oh! And unlimited soft drinks!"

"Did you say 'chicken'?"

"Nuggets! The crispy kind that kids like."

"Right," I say, blinking at her.

Back in Newton, I would have taken Harriet to the Capital Grille steakhouse, where we would have started our Christmas Eve meal with festive martinis, followed by a rich and creamy bisque, filet mignon, and a decadent dessert. Certainly not…nuggets.

"On second thought, I will pass on dinner," I say, with as much politeness as I can muster.

"Okay, then." For the first time her cheerful demeanor slips, but after a beat, her smile's right back in place. She leans forward and lowers her voice, as though to confide secrets in me. "If you like Chinese food, Golden Buddha's right across the parking lot."

"Golden Buddha?"

Still whispering, she adds, "I don't like to be disloyal, you know, to the inn. But Golden Buddha's a little more fancy 'n here. You know, cloth napkins and real glasses. And between you 'n me, they've got liquor over there too."

Practically a given that it will take quite a bit of liquor to get through the next few days, I embrace this information with gratitude.

"And," she says, more excitement creeping into her voice, "it was featured on the Food Network. Our own Golden Buddha! You know…on TV."

"You don't say."

"I wouldn't lie about something like that. It. Was. *Thrilling.*" Elf Nikki leans away and resumes her normal voice. "I'll just need a credit card to place on file, *Mrs. Kringle,* and then you can go get settled in."

"Miss," I say, taking my wallet out of my laptop bag and sliding my Platinum card across the worn countertop. "Not 'Mrs.'…ahem, Kringle. 'Miss.'"

She winks at me. "Maybe that'll change this weekend, eh? You never know. People say the North Pole is magic, and I, for one, agree!"

Her enthusiasm is relentless, and I finally surrender to it, chuckling softly. "Romance isn't on my agenda."

"Stay positive! You could go from 'Miss' to 'Mrs.' in a blink of jolly Old St. Nick's eye!" She slides a room contract to me. "I just need your signature here." With a twinge of regret, I sign the paper saying I won't burn down the place, then take my keycard from her. "You're on the second floor. Elevator's down the hallway to the right. When you get off, hang a left. Fourth door on the right is your room!"

"Thank you," I say. Even if she's a little over-the-top for my sensibilities, I have to admire Elf Nikki's commitment to the hotel's brand. "You've been very helpful."

"Have a wonderful stay in the North Pole, Miss

Kringle!" she booms as I roll my ~~eyes~~ suitcase away from her in search of my accommodations.

***

Golden Buddha is hopping.

I think every local in North Pole, Alaska, is there, plus their out-of-town guests, plus a few folks who decided to swoop down from Fairbanks too.

And I'm pleasantly surprised by the restaurant's festive decor.

First of all, the ceiling is tiled in traditional Chinese art on brass plates with an ornate recess in the center of the dining room that houses Asian-style chandeliers. I make my way to the bar, maneuvering around several waiting parties, and find it to be modern and updated. A black marble slab, popular in high-end bars all over the world, is complemented by maroon leather barstools, and a large gold Buddha holds court in a polished aluminum grotto over the cash register.

I luck out, arriving just as a man in a Denali Industrial Supply sweat shirt vacates his spot, and I belly-up, so to speak. My line of work has required me to sit alone at bars all over the world, and I have grown to love the way it feels to take my spot at the chrome or granite or marble slab, an anonymous patron in a sea of humanity. As soon as I sit down and cross my legs, a feeling of calm sweeps over me— my shoulders and posture relax for the first time in hours, and I take a deep breath, sighing softly with contentment.

Inspecting the bar's offerings, I find that they've made the unique choice to stock red wine on the three shelves to the right of the Buddha and spirits to the left. Luckily, I'm sitting on the left.

My eyes sweep the landscape for Tito's vodka, Hendrick's gin, and Glenfiddich 12 whisky, my three must-haves for any bar of any size anywhere in the world. Nodding in approval, my eyes skip around the other familiar labels, absorbing them by design without having to actually read them. There are several different kinds of rum, whiskey, and tequila, in addition to liqueurs like Midori, triple sec, Chambord, Kahlua, and schnapps. This bar tends toward the sweet, but then again, most do.

"What can I get you?"

I look up to see a young, blue-eyed waitress in a blue silk Chinese blouse, her jet-black hair back parted severely in the middle and her makeup favoring a dark, Gothic style.

"A martini, please."

"Gin or vodka?"

"Hendricks."

"Up or on the rocks?"

"Up. Icy glass."

"Olives or twist?"

Color me impressed. She knows her stuff.

"Olives. Please."

"Dry, dirty, or perfect?"

Now this is what I would call a "next-level" question, because it's asked too infrequently but perfectly addresses the drink experience you're seeking. She's good. Damn good.

"Dirty."

"You got it," she says, turning around to do her work.

I watch her add perfect measures of the ice, gin, and

olive juice to the metal shaker.

Shakeshakeshake.

She grabs an icy martini glass from a spot under the bar, pours in the clear liquid, then plops in a triple olive preset on a red plastic sword.

What's more? She presents it to me on a cocktail napkin without spilling a drop.

Honestly, it's masterful.

"Well done," I murmur.

She nods at me in acknowledgement of the compliment, then says, "Eleven dollars."

"What?"

I say this way too loudly, as evidenced by the way she breaks character and grins.

"Eleven dollars," she repeats.

Such a well-made martini would be *sixteen* dollars in Boston. Easy.

I slide a twenty-dollar bill onto the bar. "Keep the change."

Her eyes light up before she swipes it away. "Will do. Keep ordering."

Alone with my surprisingly well-made martini, I consider that although I've landed in an utterly obscure American hamlet at the northern ends of the earth, the fact that it comes outfitted with a very decent bar and an above-average bartender is gratifying. Raising the drink to my mouth, I sip gingerly, savoring the combination of flavors.

"So? What's the verdict?"

Up until now, I haven't noticed the man sitting to my

left. Now that he's facing me, I wonder if he could possibly be addressing me—he's too good-looking to be here alone on Christmas Eve, chatting up some random out-of-town woman. I look over my shoulder to see if there's someone else to my right to whom he's speaking.

"*You*," he says. "I'm talking to you. How's your martini?"

"Surprisingly excellent," I answer with a bemused grin.

He nods, laughing softly. "Brandy stumps almost everyone who orders a martini. They manage to choose between gin or vodka…most understand what she means by 'on the rocks'…and almost everyone has a preference between olives or lemons. But what separates Brandy from a run-of-the-mill bartender—"

"—is her last question!" I finish. "Most people don't know a dry martini from a perfect from a dirty."

"But I notice you ordered dirty," he says.

His voice dips just slightly as he says this, and it's just sexy enough to make the hairs on the back of my neck stand at attention and notice.

And that's not all I notice.

He's *handsome*. So very, *very* handsome in his white T-shirt and dark green "arling Farms" sweat shirt. His hair is dark and short, his eyes are green, and he's clean-shaven, which I love.

Am I ogling? Shit. I might be.

To reset the moment, I lift my drink and concentrate on taking a leisurely sip before looking up at him again. "It's perfect. She's good."

"Yes," he says. "She is."

Aha! There we go. *That's* why he's alone in a bar on Christmas Eve. He's not actually alone. I suspect that the young bartender, Brandy, might be his girlfriend. It's sweet that he's so proud of her, and I smile at him, relaxing a little. Sometimes it's easier to enjoy a truly gorgeous man when you know he's already taken.

"Where did she learn to make such a good martini?"

"Bartending school in Anchorage," he says. "She was a degenerate before that."

"I heard that!" snipes Brandy, though she doesn't break stride in pouring out six shots of something bright yellow into six small glasses. Lemon drops.

"Am I lying?" he asks her.

"No," she grouses, transferring the shots to a clean tray without looking up.

He chuckles softly. "We met a while back. I suggested she give bartending school a try."

"She could easily work in a larger bar. In a bigger city."

His eyes cool a little as he raises a lowball glass of clear liquid to his lips and sips. "But then she'd deprive the good people in North Pole of her talent."

He doesn't want her to leave. How sweet. *Definitely* her boyfriend.

"True," I say, lifting my glass. "To Brandy, the best bartender north of the Arctic Circle." "Technically, we're south, but all the same…" He grins at me, and even though he belongs to Brandy-the-bartender, a sweet shiver sluices down my spine because he's so insanely good-looking. "I'll drink to that."

I replace my glass on the napkin on the bar and offer my neighbor a friendly smile, gesturing to the logo on his sweat shirt. "So what's…'arling Farms'?"

"'Arling'? Oh!" He looks down at the cracked and worn letters that were ironed over a breast pocket long ago. He chuckles softly. "*Arling* Farms belongs to my family."

"Ah," I say. "Are you a…farmer, then?"

"I am," he says, "of sorts. Potatoes."

"I had no idea that farms could flourish this far north."

"They can," he says. "Root vegetables. Honey. Herbs. Flowers."

"Fascinating," I say, taking another sip of my very, very good martini but feeling very little of its effects. A benefit to my job? It's made my tolerance absolutely inhuman.

"Hendricks is a good gin," he says. "Do you have a favorite vodka?"

"I like Tito's on a day-to-day basis."

"But what's your *favorite*?" he asks, leaning slightly closer.

"For what?"

He thinks for a moment. "A dirty martini."

"I'd choose…Vikingfjord," I say, almost daring him to admit he's heard of it—which, of course, he hasn't. It's not well known in the United States, and I'm quite certain no one's importing it all the way to Alaska.

He raises his eyebrows.

"What?" I ask.

"Not my favorite," he answers. "It's too bitter. I prefer

a smoother model."

I blink at him. "You *know* it?"

"Of course. From Iceland. Distilled six times." His green eyes are the color of mint cream inside dark chocolate as they bite into mine. "Why do you like it?"

I inhale sharply, shifting slightly in my seat because I'm—*Jesus, what am I? Turned on? Shit. I think I just might be!* The number of men who know anything real and important about spirits and liquor is…pitifully low. The number of men in a random Chinese restaurant bar in North Pole, Alaska, who would know anything about obscure Nordic spirits? Less than zero. And yet here he is: the 0.1 percent of men appears to be my barmate.

Brandy sidles up, no doubt marking her territory. "You want another vodka, T?"

"Yeah." He doesn't slide his eyes away from mine, but his fingers connect with the lowball glass as he slides it back to her. "You didn't answer my question."

I lean away from him a touch. I don't want Brandy to think I'm on the prowl. I'm not the sort of woman who poaches a man who's already taken.

"Oh. Well, because it's cheap but usable. It's not delicious, but it's crisp. As you noted, it's bitter, yes. But the olive juice humbles it and cuts the edge."

He nods slowly, the corners of his delectable mouth tilting upward. Then with his eyes still laser-locked on mine, he asks, "What's…*delicious*?"

You. I clear my throat. "Excuse me?"

"You said that Vikingfjord isn't delicious. What is?

What would you sip?"

"Still talking vodkas?" I ask breathlessly, pulled into the vortex of his eyes like we're the only two people in the world.

"We'll get to the rest later," he promises, leaning his elbow on the bar and angling his body toward me. "Sippable vodka. What's your first pick?"

I take a deep breath.

My God, this conversation is sexy.

He's taken, I remind myself.

"There's a local one," I say lightly, "made up here in Alaska. I'm quite fond of it lately."

"What?" His eyes widen, and his flirtatious tone slips. Suddenly, he's all business. "What's it called?"

"North Star," I say.

"Your favorite vodka is North Star?" he asks, looking surprised.

I nod. "Do you know it? Artisanal. Small batch. Craft made. Traditional methods."

He leans toward me, ignoring Brandy when she slides his full glass back to him. "What do you like about it?"

"I think…well, obviously I've given it some thought, and I think it's the water they use. Up here, in Alaska, it's pure. The water can be cut from glaciers millions of years old, unaffected by the pollution of modern society. I don't know how to describe it, but it's almost"—Elf Nikki's voice rings in my ears, *People say the North Pole is magic and I, for one, agree!*—"magical."

"They have it here," he says. "Let me buy you one."

He's exceptionally good-looking, but I'm not comfortable letting a strange man buy me drinks, especially when I suspect his girlfriend is right behind the bar watching us.

"No, thank you," I say. "I'm happy with what I've got."

***

Trevor

When I decided to spend Christmas Eve at the Golden Buddha, I thought I'd just get comfortably numb in a familiar spot before heading back to my huge, lonely house.

My only goal was to get out of Fairbanks and away from my parents' house, where my twin brothers and ex-fiancée were sharing Christmas Eve dinner together. I certainly never expected to meet a woman as knowledgeable about vodka as I, let alone a woman who chooses *my* vodka as her favorite.

I'm so turned on by our conversation that I'm sitting on a barstool across from her with a half-hard cock throbbing behind the zipper of my jeans. And fuck me for being a fickle, owned-by-his-dick male, but our banter is so sexy, I'm not thinking straight. My eyes have flicked to her nude ring finger about ten times, and all I'm wondering is if she might be down to fuck when she finishes her martini.

Because I've *got* to have her.

At least once.

But preferably more.

"Brandy," I call to my protégé, ignoring my neighbor's polite refusal, "give me another. For my new friend, here."

"Lowball? North Star?"

I nod.

"Rocks?"

"Give me a break."

She grins at me. She knows exactly how I feel about ice diluting a good vodka. It should be served icy cold but not watered down.

"Coming right up, T."

I met Brandy when she was a senior in high school three years ago. I was invited, with a number of other local business owners, to speak about how I started my distillery from the ground up.

After the assembly, she came up to talk to me about getting a job in my tasting room. Though I couldn't hire her because she was only seventeen, it was clear she was smart, so I suggested she go to bartending school after graduation. When she said she couldn't afford it, I said I'd pay her way if she was serious. She took me up on it, and thus a beautiful friendship was born. She's like the kid sister I never had; I absolutely adore her.

I turn back to the woman to my right, who's refusing a drink from me.

"It's your favorite. I insist."

She looks at Brandy, then back at me. "I really don't think—"

"It's Christmastime," I wheedle.

She looks annoyed but gives me a clipped, business-like nod. "Fine."

With her dark hair slicked back into the tightest bun I've ever seen, tortoise-shell glasses covering her eyes, and no makeup, she looked like a middle-aged librarian at first glance. Dressed sensibly for Alaska in boots, jeans, and a super unsexy, bulky Irish wool sweater that completely hid her shape and curves, I clocked her arrival, but she didn't pique my interest.

It wasn't until she started talking that I started eavesdropping.

I quickly found myself hanging on her every word.

And I couldn't resist finding out if she liked the martini Brandy made for her.

Maybe it was the way she held her own as we bantered, but she got infinitely more attractive to me as we chatted.

Upon further and closer inspection, I noted the sprinkle of freckles on her nose and cheeks and the bright pink of her unpainted lips. Her eyes are a dark, deep brown behind her clunky lenses, with an attractive fringe of dark, thick eyelashes framing them.

And her smile…when she smiles at me, it feels like a gift somehow, like only a precious few are offered one, and I'm lucky enough to make the cut.

Brandy places the glass of North Star on a cocktail napkin in front of the woman. "Put it on your tab, T?"

"Thanks, Brandy." I lift my glass. "To good vodka. Cheers."

"I'm sorry, I can't." The woman sighs heavily before turning to me. "I'm *really* not comfortable accepting this."

"Why *not?*" I ask, starting to feel as annoyed as she looks.

"It's tacky," she says, gesturing to Brandy with her chin.

"I'm sure she minds when you buy drinks for other women."

"Ummm…" I glance at Brandy, who's pulling a pint of beer for a guy at the end of the bar. "Why would she mind?"

"Because you're…" She looks at Brandy, then back at me. "I mean, from the way you…I just assumed…"

My eyes widen. "You thought Brandy and I were *together*?"

"Yeah." She nods. "I do—um, I *did*?"

I laugh for a second, looking over my shoulder at a young, handsome waiter who exits the kitchen with a tray full of food. I gesture to him with my chin.

"See him?"

She twists in her chair, straining to take a look. Her sweater rides up a touch, and I get my first peek at her backside, which—I'm very happy to share—is small, rounded, and pert in tight denim.

"Uh-huh."

"That's Denny. Brandy's boyfriend."

"Ohhh." She turns back to me, her eyes wide. "So you're just…"

"A friend."

"A friend," scoffs Brandy, who's suddenly appeared across from us again. "He put me through school."

The woman's eyes slide to Brandy, then back to me. "You did?"

"He did." Brandy flattens her hands on the bar. "I was a loser kid at Lathrop High when Mr. Bigshot came to speak to the senior class about starting his own business. Said if I was serious about going to bartending school in Anchorage,

52

he'd set me up in a hotel for two weeks, give me an allowance, and pay my way. At first, I thought he was a freak, you know? Offering me money for favors I'd trade later. But nope. T just wanted to help. Got me a room at the Ramada, paid for my classes, and put in a good word with Ping to help me get this job. No favors on the side required. Just a *really* cool dude."

She raises her fist to me, and I bump it before she saunters away to help another patron.

"You paid for her education?" asks the woman, leaning closer to me.

I shrug. "She needed help. A lot of the native kids don't come from much."

"Wow." She smiles at me as she reaches for the lowball glass full of my vodka. "I really admire that."

Clinking my glass with hers, I pause a second, watching her sip because it's a beautiful fucking thing to watch a woman who knows what she's doing. Especially when it's *my* vodka she's tasting. She sips a small amount, letting it slide over her tongue as she breathes through her nose. Her eyes flutter closed for a moment, and her lips tilt up with approval before she nods, straightening up to look at me.

As for me? That semi in my pants is quickly becoming a full-blown hard-on. Because if that preorgasmic sip of my vodka wasn't the hottest fucking thing I've ever seen, I don't know what is.

"Delicious," she hums, her voice low and silky.

"Who *are* you?" I whisper.

"Faye," she says, holding out her hand. "And

you're…T, the bigshot potato farmer."

I could correct her slightly erroneous description of me—I'm actually Trevor, the bigshot distillery owner—but I don't feel like giving her my résumé. I don't want to risk changing the vibe of our conversation if she finds out the vodka she loves is one of mine. Besides, I grew up on a working potato farm. It's not really a lie, and if it is, it's little and white.

I take her small, freckled hand in mine, clasping the delicate bones as I stare into her eyes. "Nice to meet you, Faye."

"Nice to meet you, T."

I pump her hand for a second or two, then let go. But only because it would be creepy if I held onto her any longer.

"You're from out of town," I say.

"Mm-hm."

"Why are you here?"

She chuckles softly. "Can't a girl spend Christmas in the North Pole?"

"Sure," I murmur, wishing she was spending Christmas on *my* pole instead. "No family?"

Shit. As soon as the words come out of my mouth, I wish I could take them back. A shadow passes over her face, and she finishes off her martini in a way that feels driven by emotion, not pleasure.

"Not today," she finally whispers, sliding the martini glass back toward Brandy and pulling the lowball glass forward. She looks up at me. "You?"

"Not from out of town," I say.

"Family?"

I lean closer to her, borrowing her own words. "Not today."

"Two foundlings all alone at the holidays," she observes. "Whatever shall we do?"

Hmm. If that's a come-on, I'm game.

I don't want to get *involved* with her, of course, but we both appear to be available. She could be the perfect person with whom to spend the next few days before I hook up with Faith Crawford over New Year's. I'm a free agent, right? I don't owe any woman anything. I can do what I want to, and if that includes fucking a beautiful librarian in North Pole for three days before fucking a beautiful sailor in Fairbanks the following weekend, more power to me.

"Faye," I say, "—after you finish your drink, of course—would you like to get out of here?"

She stares at me for a long second. "No thank you."

Cue the sound effect of a needle skipping over a record.

"Wait. *What?*" I feel my brows furrow. I think I'm frowning at her. "Did you say no?"

"I can't," she says.

"What do you mean you can't?"

Am I pouting? I think I might be.

"I have plans…" she says, looking away from me.

Is it my imagination, or does she seem the slightest bit sorry that she has plans?

"Tonight?"

"Not exactly, but…"

She clears her throat, like she's not sure what else to

say.

"Some plans were made to be broken," I say, trying to keep my voice light.

She shakes her head then adds, "It's complicated."

"It always is," I say, adjusting on my seat and telling my dick that it appears he's going to have to wait for some action...not that it helps. He wants what he wants, and what he wants is her.

"So that's it?" I ask her.

"No." Her shoulders hug her ears in a brief shrug, and she gives me a little smile. "It doesn't have to be."

"What does that mean?"

"When you suggested we 'get out of here,' you were suggesting we have sex, right?"

My cheeks flush because she says this so matter-of-factly, and it embarrasses me that I made such a bold suggestion to a woman I barely know. But she's calling me out, and I'm not a coward, so despite my shame, I nod.

"I can't have sex with you," she says. "But..."

"But what?"

"Well...we could have some dinner...and talk about the world's best vodkas over decent-smelling Chinese food," she suggests, gesturing to an open table in the back restaurant, and then looking back at me with hope in her eyes.

"Why?"

"Because we're human beings," she says softly, "alone at Christmastime. And I think we both deserve better than that."

There's something about her honesty that tugs at my heartstrings that makes me want to rescue both of us from a night of loneliness, but Marlena's face flashes through my mind, and I put a swift end to those thoughts. I don't want a friend. I don't want a relationship. I want no depth, no connection, no nothing.

And something about Faye *already* feels deeper and more connected to me than it should. I'm *feeling* something just talking to her, and I don't want to. In fact, if I'm honest in a way that aches, it scares me that I could develop feelings—any feelings—for another woman. I need to stay cold. Cool. Emotionless. I need to protect myself.

So if a little fun in the form of meaningless sex isn't in the cards...I guess it's time to go.

I pick up my drink, finish it, then replace the glass on the bar with a dull clunk. Sliding off the barstool, I take a one-hundred-dollar bill from my wallet and put it under my cocktail napkin. Then I turn to Faye.

"Enjoy your drink. I'm going to head out."

"Wait. You mean—oh." Her face falls. "You're leaving."

"Afraid so."

Though I wish it didn't, the disappointment in her eyes twists my heart.

"Really?"

Hurt joins disappointment and I waver, but my still-broken heart cautions me: *Stay cool, Trevor. Stay cold.*

"Really," I say as nonchalantly as I can manage. "Nothing left to stay for."

"Oh." She blinks rapidly, then clenches her jaw and lifts her chin. "Okay."

"You have a good night," I say lightly, forcing my feet to move away from her toward the exit and trying to convince myself as I go that it's for the best.

CHAPTER FOUR

Faye

The abruptness with which T leaves me is strangely and unexpectedly devastating—like a surprise smack across the face that whips your neck back and leaves an angry red mark on your cheek.

It stings.

As he saunters away, I find myself in unfamiliar territory, blinking my eyes furiously, embarrassed and confused, desperately willing myself not to cry. But today has been full of disappointments, and I just don't have much morale left.

Not to mention, I feel stupid. *So* stupid.

And since it's an unusual feeling for me, I don't have the tools to deal with it, which makes me feel even *more* off-balance.

The reality is that I'm not experienced with men. I'm not a good judge of them on a personal level (*clearly*). I would have sworn on a stack of Bibles that T and I were *connecting*, but obviously we weren't. That exciting feeling that we "got" each other was me misreading the situation like some starry-eyed teenager. It's a reminder that I'm woefully lacking in any fragment of adult female intuition, a realization that makes me feel deeply ashamed.

It also hurts my feelings that his *only* interest in me was physical. The rest of it—the conversation, the banter, the smiles and flirtation—was all a play to get into my pants. I had been building meaning into our exchange, when he only saw me as a piece of ass.

It all feels…*dreadful*.

I scramble for my purse, eager to pay up my tab and run back to my motel, but I'm so flustered it takes a moment for me to realize my tab is all paid for. Placing my hand flat on the bar to steady myself as I slide off my barstool, I'm surprised when it's suddenly covered by another.

"It's not you. It's him."

I look up into Brandy's face, then flick my eyes to where her hand is gently holding the back of mine.

"S-Sorry?"

"It's not you. It's him." She squeezes lightly, then pulls her hand away. "He got worked over by his fiancée a few months ago. It left him…bitter."

"Worked over?"

"Yeah. Um…you know what?" She glances at the clock sitting over the Buddha's head. "I have a thirty-minute break coming up. Wanna grab something to eat? It tastes as good as it smells. I promise."

Split between a desire to run back to cry myself to sleep or to mollify my hurt feelings by learning more about T's sordid past, my curiosity—and hunger—win out.

"Are you sure?" I ask her, assuming she has better things to do on Christmas Eve than share dinner with a total stranger.

"Positive. I'm starving."

"Well, in that case, it's my treat," I tell her.

"Ooh! Even better!" Brandy grins at me, then calls to her fellow bartender. "Jim, I'm taking my thirty."

"No way! It's busy here, Brandy!"

"Then work harder, Jim!" she bellows back, untying her white apron and placing it under the register before exiting the bar through a hinged counter.

I eye the drink T bought me but decide I need to find a new favorite vodka, and I leave it on the bar unfinished, following Brandy to an open booth in the back of the restaurant. We sit down on red leather bench seats across from each other, and she hands me a menu.

"Mind if I get the Mongolian beef?" she asks. "It's epic."

"How about this?" I slide the menu back to her. "You order for us."

"Really? Yeah. Sure!" She grins. "Are you hungry?"

"Famished."

The waiter T pointed out to me before comes over to our table and leans down to kiss Brandy on the cheek before offering me his hand.

"I'm Denny."

"Faye."

"Saw you over at the bar talking to T."

Brandy clears her throat. "He's being an asshole tonight."

"What else is new?" asks Denny.

"Cut it out," says Brandy, eyeing her boyfriend sharply. "Give him a break, huh? He's not like that. Not really. He's a good guy going through a rough time."

"Whatever you say, babe." He shrugs, taking his notepad out of his white apron and looking at me. "What'cha having?"

"Faye's having a scorpion bowl to start," says Brandy.

"Which one?"

"North Pole Paradise."

I clear my throat. "What is a scor—"

Brandy hushes me with a flick of her hand, then continues: "I'll have a Sapporo. Then bring us the crab rangoon and ahi tuna, followed by the Mongolian beef and velvet shrimp."

Denny grimaces. "Babe, rent's due on—"

"Faye's treating."

He brightens instantly. "Oh! Awesome. Cool. Anything else?"

"A shot of tequila," I say.

"Bring her a shot of 1800 Silver," says Brandy.

"Salt?" he asks. "Lemon?"

Brandy slides her eyes to me, and after a beat, we both giggle.

"Fuck, Brandy," gripes Denny. "You could just say no. You don't have to laugh at me."

"Don't be so sensitive," she says. "You know the rule: when it comes to shots, take 'em neat. Don't dilute and don't pollute."

"Yeah, yeah, yeah," he says, rolling his eyes as he

gathers our menus and heads to the bar and kitchen to place our orders.

I watch her watch him go, taking in the soft look on her otherwise hard face. When she turns back to me, I'm smile at her.

"You love him," I say.

"I do, but he's an idiot."

"Is he?"

She shrugs. "Sorta. But he loves me back and lets me be in charge."

"Is that important to you? To be in charge in a relationship?" I pause for a second. "I always thought women wanted to be taken care of."

"Ha!" she scoffs. "'Taken care of' is great as long as you have the littlest, tiniest bit of an upper hand. Put it this way: always make sure your man loves you just a *little* more than you love him." She holds up her hand leaving a hair's width of space between her thumb and index finger. "Just a *tiny* bit. Just enough to know that you're safe."

"Safe?"

"If you're more important to him than he is to you—even if it's only by a miniscule amount—you won't have to worry about him cheating or leaving you or being mean. When you've got your period and you're acting like a bitch, he'll cut you a break. When you get fat from having babies, he'll still think you're beautiful. Only stay with a guy who's crazy about you." She takes a gulp of water and shrugs. "Anyway, that's the advice my mother gave me, and she and my dad have been together for a hundred years."

I fold my hands together and stare at her in wonder.

"How old are you?" I ask.

"Twenty-one." Her phone is sitting on the table and buzzes. "Do you mind if I take this? It's my dad."

"Go ahead."

She presses the phone to her ear. "*Seya?*"

She continues to speak in a language unknown to me while I busy myself with placing a napkin on my lap and take a moment to marvel about how self-assured Brandy is in her personal life and how knowledgeable she is about men.

At twenty-one years old, she seems to have the opposite sex all figured out. And here I am, almost a decade older, and I can't get through a conversation with a random man at a bar without getting my feelings hurt.

How did that happen?

I prop my elbow on the table and lean my cheek on my knuckles.

Maybe I was just a "late bloomer," more interested in academics than boys for most of my formative years. I never had a "boy crazy" phase like many of my peers. I barely noted the opposite sex as different, actually, except to observe that they were sometimes given unfair advantages in sports, which grated on my refined sense of justice and equality.

During high school and college, I was so focused on my course of study and grades, I made no room in my life for boys. Why? They simply weren't a priority. I spent every waking hour studying at the library or shutting down at the computer lab. And by the time I entered grad school, I was grieving my lost parents, trying to maintain my perfect GPA and make important decisions about my little sister's future. After grad school, I took the reins of my father's business in hand and worked as hard at keeping Findley Imports above water as I had at keeping my grades straight As.

To my immense pleasure, I succeeded. I worked my ass off and made Findley Imports one of the largest and most profitable private spirit importation companies in the United States.

Except…

Now that I find myself with a successful company and space in my life for a meaningful relationship, I don't know how to find one. I have friends, but I'm lonely for someone special. I want a husband and children someday. I just don't know how to navigate my way through meeting someone, let alone through courtship and love. Hand me a spreadsheet or a marketing plan, and I'm a whiz. Sit me down at the bar beside an attraction, intelligent man, and I'm a dodo.

At some point, I'll need to figure out how an accomplished businesswoman goes about meeting the love of her life, but there is *one* thing I want to take care of first:

My virginity.

I *want* to get rid of it.

(I am literally dying to get rid of it.)

I don't *want* to be a virgin anymore.

Since answering Mr. Fairbanks' ad two weeks ago and receiving an answer last week informing me that I was his chosen New Year's date, I've avoided the topic of my virginity with myself, though it circles in my mind like a vulture circling fresh kill.

So here we go.

As I'm waiting for something called a scorpion bowl to arrive while having Christmas Eve dinner at a Chinese restaurant in North Pole, Alaska, with a virtual stranger, I realize it's time.

Let's go, Faye. Let's face it.

My maidenhood.

My v-card.

MY VIRGINITY.

I probably should have lost it back in high school or college—or at some point in my twenties, at least. But for all my left-brain dominance, I had some pretty dreamy notions about my "first time." Minimally, I wanted to be in love with my first partner, and since I've never even come close to falling in love, I suppose sex never entered the equation.

Now here I am, thirty years old, and clearing three decades on this earth without being intimate with a man makes me feel...embarrassed, inexperienced...like I'm missing out on something that I should have tried long before now.

Not to mention, the longer you wait, I've learned, the more society pegs you as a weirdo with a dirty secret. And I don't want to feel like that anymore either.

But all that's going to change now.

I don't care if I'm in love or not. I don't care if I never see Mr. Fairbanks again after New Year's weekend. I know it's probably going to hurt physically, but so does a root canal, and I've borne that pain without making a scene.

If I don't want to downsize my family-sized house or live the rest of my life like a spinster, I need to do *something* drastic to jumpstart my exploration of men and desire and my body and my latent sexuality. If I don't, I fear I never will.

Plus, the businesslike tone and quality of his ad appealed to me.

He wants a date for New Year's? Well, I want to lose my virginity. *Quid pro quo.* We'll both get what we want.

Do I have some misgivings about the fact that I'll be a virgin the first time I ever have sex with a virtual stranger?

Yes. Of course I do. Three decades of not sharing my body with anyone else hasn't exactly made me free-spirited, but I will just approach this with the same sort of head-on, can-do determination that helps me succeed in business. I know how the deed is done. Part A of Person A is inserted into Part A of Person B. Person A thrusts his hips in a forward motion repeatedly until—

"One North Pole scorpion bowl…and one tequila shot."

I'm startled by Denny's return to our table and look up at him in surprise as he lowers a neat shot of tequila and a large—*maybe thirty-two ounces?*—bowl of liquid to the table, complete with several brightly colored straws.

I pick up the much-needed shot and let the smooth tequila glide down my throat before gesturing to the *vat* of liquid he's placed between me and Brandy. "What is this?"

"Scorpion bowl," he says.

"Right. But what's in it?"

"Nope! Don't tell her!" Brandy places her phone on the table and shifts her glance to me. "You have to taste it and tell me."

I stare at the reddish-purple liquid for a second, then frown at her. "I'm not accustomed to drinking things that I—"

"Just try it already," she says. She fingers a hot-pink straw for a second before leaning forward to take a big sip, after which she smacks her lips dramatically. "Delicious."

I choose a bright aqua straw and lean forward, clasping it between my lips and drinking until the sour sweetness fills my mouth and puckers my lips. "Oh!"

"Like it?"

"Um…" *Do I like it?* Honestly, I'm not sure. "What is it?"

"You tell me," says Brandy.

I take another sip, and another, and really, Brandy is correct. It *is* delicious.

"Vodka."

"What kind?" asks Brandy.

"Absolut Citron."

"Damn, you're good," she tells me. "What else?"

"Hendrick's?"

"Your favorite," says Brandy, leaning forward to take another sip. "Anything else?"

I take a gulp this time, letting the flavors combine on my tongue and sighing with satisfaction. "Sake, cranberry juice, fresh lemon, fresh lime, mint, and…cucumber?"

"Impressive," says Brandy. "But you're missing one

thing."

"What?"

"A liqueur, but I won't tell you what it is," she says. "Keep drinking. You'll figure it out."

Every gulp goes down smoother than the last until the bowl is one-third gone.

Pausing from my drink, I look around the restaurant, and I decide that it's the most festive place I've visited in...years. And Brandy? My goodness, she is just a pip. How lucky that I managed to bump into her tonight! Things are looking better already.

I grin at her. "Hey! Weren't you going to tell me about T? How he got 'worked over'?"

"Yeah." She nods. "Sure. Okay."

"He's hot," I hear myself say, "for a farmer."

"Hey!" Brandy tilts her head to the side and raises her eyebrows. "Can't farmers be hot?"

Oh shit! Why did I say that aloud? I glance at the scorpion bowl. Hmm. This is probably a lot of alcohol, even for me. But it's too good to stop sipping, so I don't.

"Farmers can *definitely* be hot, as evidenced by T," I say. "But between you and me? He didn't look like a farmer. Not at all. I'm skeptical that he even *is* a farmer. He had a—hmm, I don't know...like, a clean-cut businessman thing going on."

"Yeah," says Brandy. "I guess he does. In fairness, he also started a—"

"Don't be fair!" I demand, leaning forward a little, unable to politely curb my curiosity anymore. "Just spill the beans."

"Spill the beans, huh? Drink up, Faye," she advises with a chuckle. "You're getting fun." She takes another sip of her beer, then folds her hands on the table. "Okay…so, here's the deal: T was dating this girl, Marlena, who was a nurse at the local hospital. They got together right around the time I got the job here, and I was eighteen, so I guess they had been together for about three years when he popped the question last February. Gorgeous couple. Totally in love…or so we thought."

"Dun…dun…duuuuuun," I intone dramatically.

"Oh man. Are you getting drunk?" Brandy snorts through a giggle. "Anyway, he heads down to Portland in June—that's where she's from—to get married…Only to find out she'd been having an affair with his brother! For months."

"Stop it!" I yell, hugging the large bowl to my chest with my pink straw lodged in the pouch of my cheek so I can sip while I talk. Everything's far more efficient this way. "That's horrible!"

"Mm-hm. She's a regular cunt."

"Language!" I scold, shaking my head with disapproval at Brandy's dirty mouth.

"Language," she scoffs. "Did anyone ever tell you that you're a trip?"

"Keeeeeeeep…g-going!" I manage to sputter through sips and swallows and the straw I'm still holding between my lips so I can mainline this concoction.

"So he comes back to Alaska with his heart in tatters.

70

Didn't get married, of course. And he's extra heartbroken, because he loves Cez—"

"Who?"

"Cez. With a z. His younger brother, Cecil."

"His brother's name is Cecil?"

"Is that important?"

"It's just unusual."

Sweet Christ, I've never had anything as yummy as what I'm drinking right this second. I'm going to order another and another and—

"Anyway, there's more."

"What?" My eyes are bugging out of my head. I just know it.

"Then he finds out Marlena is pregnant," she says, making a hand motion like a bomb exploding. "Bam!"

"No!" I say, spitting scorpion punch all over the table. And damn it, that's a shame, because I really don't want to waste it.

"Yes," says Brandy, laughing as she uses her napkin to wipe down the tabletop. "Hey, you might want to slow down a little."

"No way. This is the best drink ever."

She narrows her eyes. "How often do you mix alcohols?"

"Never," I say. "Never ever. Never ever ever." I giggle. "Don't dilute, don't pollute."

Just then, Denny reappears with food, and I swear I'm hungry, but at the same time, this drink is all I need to be happy until the world stops spinning. I'm positive. And sadly, it's almost gone.

"Bring me another," I tell him.

"Another shot?"

"Another scorpion bowl!"

"Uhh…" He darts his eyes at Brandy, who shrugs as she piles her plate with food. He looks back at me. "Are you sure? It's a lot."

"Yep! I'm in love with it."

He grins at me. "O-kaaaay. Whatever you say."

Denny leaves to squeeze more nectar from the tits of the gods while I finish off the scorpion bowl and smile at my dinner partner. Looking at her, it occurs to me that Brandy and Harriet are about the same age, but it's so much easier to talk to Brandy. Why is that? Why are Harriet and I always so stiff and awkward together? Why can't I sit across a table from Harriet and talk about hot men who've been jilted? Why couldn't *we* drink scorpion bowls and have a proper giggle?

"I wish my sister was more like you," I say.

"You barely know me."

"I barely know her."

"Maybe that's the problem."

"Maybe," I say, feeling a little sad when I think of Harriet in Vail.

"Are you getting sad? Don't get sad on me. Eat something," suggests Brandy.

"I'm fine. Finish the story."

"Not much else to say," she says, biting into another Rangoon. "Oh, except…now they're engaged too. Cez and

Marlena. Engaged *and* having a baby. And T—well, he's all alone."

"Oh, Brandy…" Still hugging the almost-cached scorpion bowl to my chest, I feel tears flood my eyes. My lips quiver. "That's…that's so saaaaad."

"Lord, you're not a weepy drunk, are you? Ugh." She cringes, then shrugs, sliding the last clean napkin to me. "Wouldn't have guessed that."

"I d-don't know," I sob, blowing my runny nose. "I d-don't get d-drunk, so I w-wouldn't know."

"Sure you don't," she says, then adds again, "Eat something."

I take a wonton and shove it into my mouth. "I'm…sho…shorry…for T."

"Yeah," she says. "Me too." She sighs. "He wasn't nice to you tonight, but he's not an asshole at heart. I promise. He's a good guy going through a shitty time."

Denny appears like a messenger from heaven and swaps out my scorpion bowls just in the nick of time. I choose the yellow straw this time and suck on it like scorpion bowls are about to be obliterated from the face of the earth.

"Are you *sure* you want more?" Brandy asks me, her eyes wide as she stares at the full bowl of alcohol and juices. "I think you're going to hurt tomorrow, Faye."

Pish posh. Yes, yes, I do want more. I want as much as I want, and I think that's a lot.

As I swallow, I'm *finally* able to identify the ingredient that eluded me with the last batch.

"Elderflower liqueur!" I yell in victory.

Brandy chuckles and nods. "Whoop! There it is."

***

Trevor

I am *such* an asshole.

Jesus. When did I become such a fucking asshole?

I'm sitting in my car outside of the Golden Buddha, trying to decide whether to go home or to go back inside, and it's been almost half an hour now. I've been watching the door carefully, and she hasn't come out, though I don't know what I'd do if she suddenly appeared. Although I owe her an apology, it would be creepy as fuck to suddenly approach her in the dark parking lot after treating her like garbage at the bar. And yet, I can't seem to turn the key in the ignition and leave either.

All I know is that right this second, I'm ashamed of myself.

That woman—Faye—was nothing but nice.

Better than nice, even: she was ethical. She didn't touch that drink I bought her until she knew that Brandy and I weren't a couple. She was *better* and more decent than most women.

All alone in a strange town on Christmas Eve, I could see it took some courage for her to suggest we have dinner. I could see the flush of her cheeks and the hope in her eyes, and what did I do? I purposely hurt her feelings. Why? Because some other woman totally unconnected to Faye broke my heart? Well, that's no excuse. I had no right to make her feel like shit.

Especially because we'd had a nice conversation.

Better than nice. *Fuck nice.*

Electric.

I bang on the steering wheel twice, hard, then take a deep breath and exhale slowly.

I'm pissed off, because it's one thing to protect *myself*, but it's another to hurt *someone else*. Someone innocent. Someone who has nothing to do with the shit Marlena put me through. It's wrong. Stupid wrong. It's not the sort of person I want to be.

Not to mention, I don't *need* to pick up random women in bars. I have Faith Crawford coming into town in five short days for a weekend of no-strings-attached hot sex. I don't need anyone else. I literally have the perfect situation already set up to meet my needs. I don't know what happened in there. I got carried away, I guess. I was attracted to her and acted like a total asshole by clumsily propositioning her and then leaving when she wasn't interested. Ugh. Gross.

I catch a glimpse of myself in the rearview mirror and stare back with loathing at my reflection.

"You're such a dick," I tell myself, shaking my head.

Shit. What if she's in the bathroom weeping right now because I'm a fucking dick? I need to go back inside and apologize. I need to tell her that I'm sorry for treating her like a whore. I need to tell her that *she's* beautiful and interesting and *I'm* a fucking mess.

It's not you, I'll tell her. *It's me.*

I unbuckle my seat belt and exit the car, walking briskly

back into the restaurant. Ping sees me return and waves at me from the dining room, but I beeline to the bar. Standing behind the row of stools, I realize that not only is Faye no longer sitting there, but someone else has taken her place.

Did I miss her? Did I somehow miss her leaving the bar?

No. I was watching the door carefully. Even when I was glancing with revulsion at my face in the mirror, I still had my peripheral vision locked on the Golden Buddha. So…where is she? Using my full height—six foot three inches—to look over the glass barriers that section off parts of the dining room, I comb through the tables. *No. No. No…Shit. Where is she?* I step out of the bar area to get a better look around and—

"Hey T."

"Hi Denny," I say, glancing to my left.

"Looking for someone?" he asks.

When I look over, his face is slightly pissy. I don't think Denny's ever liked me. I think he's always been suspicious that I had ulterior motives for helping Brandy with school. But he'd be wrong about that.

"Yeah," I say, still checking out the various tables. I see a redheaded woman toward the back and wonder if—

"Faye?" asks Denny. "You lookin' for Faye?"

My eyes jerk to his. "Yeah."

Denny purses his lips. "Why don't you leave it alone?"

I cross my arms over my chest. "Is she still here?"

"Yeah," says Denny, his shoulders drooping. He's bigger than me by at least forty pounds, but Denny's a lover, not a fighter. "She's sitting in the way back with Brandy."

"Thanks," I say, brushing by him to go make my amends.

It's not you, it's me.

It's not you, it's me.

I try it out in various voices and tones in my head, finally settling on firm and direct, without too much self-pity for me or too much sympathy for her.

When I circle around the last booth in a row of five, I'm ready to say my piece, except I stop in my tracks when I hear a whoop of laughter, followed by a series of inelegant snorts. What stops me is that I know Brandy's laugh, and it's not Brandy who's laughing. Which means it must be…Faye.

Since she's obviously not crying her eyes out in the bathroom, I consider leaving this alone and going back to my car, but I can't help myself. I want to see Faye again. I want to apologize.

I slow down a little, clearing an ornate column to find Brandy sitting at her favorite booth, facing me.

"T," she says, raising one pierced eyebrow when she notices me. "You're back."

"No, he's not!" exclaims Faye. "He left, remember?"

I step around the back of the booth so that I'm facing the table. Brandy's sitting back a little, her plate mostly clean. Faye—who when I left her thirty minutes ago looked like a kicked kitten—is hugging a scorpion bowl to her chest, with two fluorescent straws rising from the bowl and disappearing into the corners of her mouth.

She looks up at me, blinks twice in surprise, then

smiles.

"T," she says gently, her voice filled with wonder as she lifts her head, bringing the straws with her like walrus tusks. "It's you."

"It's him, alright," says Brandy, her lips tilting up in a sardonic smile. "Forget something?"

"No. I mean…yeah." I run my hand through my hair. "I wanted to talk to Faye…to um, apolog—"

"Brandy!" yells Jim from the bar. "Get back here—now!"

Jim's demand, bellowed from across the room, makes Faye's eyes widen before she bursts into unrestrained laughter.

"He's so…loud!" she cackles with glee, lowering her straws back into the bowl and closing her eyes as she sips.

Brandy grins at her dinner companion before sliding out of the booth.

"I have to go back to work, Faye. Thanks for dinner. You rock."

Faye opens her eyes halfway. "Nope. *You*…rock."

For no good reason whatsoever, this makes her start laughing again.

Brandy leans into me as she stands up, whispering, "She's loaded. Don't let her drink anything else. And make sure she gets home safe."

"Where's home?"

"The inn."

Brandy backs away, her eyes conveying a clear message that if I upset Faye or try anything remotely ungentlemanly,

I'll be answering to her, and it won't be pretty. For someone so young and only a little over five feet tall, Brandy is legit terrifying sometimes.

"I'll get her back in one piece," I whisper back.

She turns around. "Faye, don't forget what I said: come back tomorrow at four. My folks'll be here. Denny's too. It's a big family dinner. Anyone's welcome. *You're* welcome."

"Yummmmy!" says Faye, waggling her fingers in farewell. "Thanks...Brandy."

"You should come too," Brandy tells me as she heads back to the bar.

"I'll think about it," I mutter before sitting down in her empty seat.

Faye's still hugging the bowl, her chin resting on the rim, and her eyes closed. I only know she's drinking because of the light slurping sound I can hear coming from her mouth. I would've guessed she had more of a tolerance. A scorpion bowl is thirty-two ounces of mixed alcohol, and by my calculations, she's had half of that. *She can't handle sixteen ounces?*

"How's your drink?" I ask her.

One eye pops open, but she's otherwise still. "The second's as good as the first."

The second? "You're on your second...*bowl?*"

"Uh-huh," she murmurs. "An' Ima have a third one if I want."

No, you're not.

Okay, this is making more sense now. She's had about—*forty? Forty-eight?*—ounces of mixed alcohol in about the same number of minutes. Fuck. I mean, I know they put juices and shit in the bowl along with the alcohol, but she's still had a lot.

"Youuu…," she says, pointing a finger at me, "are *not*…very *nice*."

I nod. "You're right."

"We were…jus' talk-een," she says, raising her head again. I'm tempted to pull the straws out of her mouth because she looks so ridiculous, but I'm worried I'll offend her, so they stay where they are, the brightly colored fluorescent tusks bobbing in my direction as she speaks. "D'you wanna have dinner? No ma'am! Jus' sex."

I clear my throat. "I know that—"

"You know…*nothing*," she says. One straw falls out and bounces on the table before falling on the floor. She's left with one and looks sadly lopsided now. "I'm very tired."

"Are you?"

"Yes, I am. I left Newark at ten o'clock this morning and—" Suddenly, her eyebrows furrow, and she frowns. "And I…I don' feel so…so well…uhhhhg…"

"How about we get some air?" I suggest.

It takes her a second to fully lift her head and focus her eyes on mine. "Air. Yeah. I need some air…"

Before I can stand up, she slides out of the booth in a hurry, leaving her coat behind. I grab it, following her weaving path past a row of booths and out the front door.

CHAPTER FIVE

Trevor

By the time I catch up with her, she's standing in the parking lot, one hand braced on the nearest SUV, head bent over, and the contents of one-and-a-half scorpion bowls heaving forth onto the snow in shades of reddish-purple.

She retches over and over again, four or five times, gasping for breath between each bout. Her back rises and falls rapidly as she waits for a final expulsion, but it doesn't come. Finally, she stands up, turns around, and leans back against the truck.

"God," she half-murmurs, half-sobs. "Oh God. What a mess."

I would've offered to hold her hair back, but her bun's doing a better job than I ever could. Not a single hair is loose.

"Can I, um—get you anything? Water? A...tissue?"

She looks up at me, her eyes glistening with tears, and backhands her mouth with the sleeve of her wool sweater. "No. Thanks."

"The good news is that you just got most of the poison out. You'll feel a lot better in a little bit."

"What's...the bad news?" she asks, looking up at me

with bleary eyes.

"I get to walk you back to your hotel."

"I don't n-need"—she places her hand over her mouth like she might vomit again, then lowers it slowly when she doesn't—"an...escort."

"I'll keep my distance," I promise her.

"Why should I believe you?" she mutters. "You made your...*intentions* clear earlier."

"I was a total ass," I tell her.

"No argument here," she says, taking a deep breath of cold air. She stares at me for a second, looking tired and miserable, and I realize I'm still holding her coat. I offer it to her.

"I'm very sorry," I say, "for the way I treated you before."

"You *should* be," she mumbles, shrugging into her coat.

"And I'd feel better about everything if I knew you got home safe."

"*You* feeling better about everything isn't my first priority," she says, side-eyeing me.

"C'mon. I'll be on my best behavior from now on. I promise."

She takes another deep breath, looks at the motel, which is a quarter mile across a very dark and empty parking lot, then back at me. "Fine. Let's go."

After she zips up her coat, she crosses her arms over her chest and starts walking without looking at me. Gone is the sophisticated, well-spoken woman from the bar. Now? She's just a young woman in a strange town who had way too much to drink way too fast.

"So, uh…" I say as our boots crunch over the snow and ice, "did you say you flew in from New York today?"

"I had a meeting in Manhattan this morning, but I actually left from Newark."

It takes me a second to get my head around this, not only because New York is so far away but also because I can't imagine why she would fly from New York to Fairbanks on Christmas Eve.

"Have family in the area?"

"We already covered that," she says.

Shit. Right. We did. And it was a sore spot the first time. *Great job, Trev.*

"So…you're just checking out Alaska for Christmas, huh?"

"Sort of," she says. She takes a deep breath, then adds, "There's a business my company is interested in acquiring, and it's located in Fairbanks, so I thought I'd spend Christmas in the North Pole and then try to meet with the owner the day after."

"I know just about every business owner in Fairbanks," I tell her. "It's a small town."

"I believe that."

"So if you wanted to…"

"What?"

"Tell me about it—um, your deal. Maybe I could give you some pointers on the personalities in play."

She glances up at me. "Why would you do that?"

I shrug. "Because I'm not as much of an asshole as I

acted like back there."

"No offense, but I'm not really in the mood to talk business…"

"Yeah," I say. "I get it."

We walk in silence for several minutes before she speaks again.

"Brandy told me about your, um…" She clears her throat. "Your brother."

This surprises me because Brandy isn't much of a gossip, so she really must have taken issue with my behavior if she made excuses for me. "What exactly did she say?"

"Just that you were engaged and…it didn't work out."

"That's the G-rated version," I mutter.

"I'm really sorry," she says. "I can't imagine how much that must have hurt."

I reach behind my neck with a bare hand and rub the skin there. I'm uncomfortable discussing this on one hand, but on the other, the polite sympathy in her voice feels…nice. I haven't talked about this with anyone in a while. I've sort of been dealing with it on my own.

"Yeah. It sucked."

"To be clear," she says, "I don't think it gives you the right to be a jerk to strange women, but 'to understand all is to forgive all.'"

Forgive. It's such an old-fashioned word, and yet it holds so much power.

"Do you forgive me?" I ask her.

She nods as we stop on the sidewalk by the front door of the hotel. When she raises her head, her dark eyes seize mine, searching them for a moment before saying, "Yes. I do."

Most of the time when people offer forgiveness or acceptance, it's not wholehearted. It's a way of smoothing over an uncomfortable situation, while remnants of hurt are still actively alive in the equation. That's why Faye's face—the softness around her intelligent eyes and openness of her expression—is so extraordinary in this moment. Because I sense that understanding, compassion, and forgiveness mean something real to this person. She has cleaned the proverbial slate between us, and there is no lingering ill will.

Furthermore, I sense that the open road that lay before us while we sat at the bar an hour ago is now, miraculously, restored. And for me, to me, it feels like a gift. That is the only way I can explain it.

"Thank you," I whisper.

"You're welcome," she answers.

"Home safe and sound," I say, gesturing to the facade of the hotel. "As promised."

Her lips tilt up a touch. "*Home* may be taking things too far."

"How will you spend tomorrow?" I ask her.

"I don't know yet," she says. "Brandy invited me for dinner at the Golden Buddha, so I'll probably end up there."

"I've been to Christmas dinner there before," I tell her. "It's lots of fun."

"Will you be there tomorrow?" she asks.

Will I be there tomorrow?

Ping invites me every year, but I hadn't planned to be

this year.

I'd planned to be at my parents' house for the entire day, sharing brunch and opening gifts, watching movies or a game, and sharing dinner together. But now I'm not sure.

As much as I'm not interested in getting involved with anyone, I'm undeniably intrigued by this woman who left New York this morning, knows a lot about vodka, and decided to spend Christmas in a strange town all by herself. I wish I could know her—or maybe just know more *about* her. All I really know is that I would be unaccountably sorry to leave her here with no plan to ever see her again.

"Maybe," I whisper, feeling off-kilter but not minding the feeling as much as I probably should.

"Then *maybe* I'll see you there," she says, holding out her hand to me.

I reach forward with mine, and slowly, gently, we embrace one another's hands, skin to skin, flesh to flesh, strangely intimate and yet culturally appropriate. Her hand, as I noted before, is small, warm, and freckled, and I savor the contact even more the second time around.

"It was nice to meet you," I tell her. I want to apologize again, but I know it's unnecessary. She's already forgiven me for my very bad behavior.

"It was"—she pauses for a second before pulling her hand away, an attractive blush pinkening her cheeks—"certainly interesting. Good night."

She turns and walks into the hotel, disappearing down the back hallway toward the elevator. And I stand there, out in the cold, watching her go until I can't see her anymore.

***

It's a twenty-five minute drive from the Golden Buddha to my house, and my phone rings while I'm driving home.

"Hello?"

"Hey," says Baz.

"What's up?"

"You didn't come."

"I told you I wouldn't."

"It hurt Mom's feelings."

Hearing this pinches my heart because I love my mother. But it also pinches my heart because she knows how I feel about Cez and Marlena, and she invited them for Christmas Eve anyway. Even though I know it wasn't her intention, it almost feels like she chose them over me.

"That's too bad, but she had to know I wouldn't be there."

"I think she hoped that you'd show up anyway, it being Christmas Eve and all."

"Baz—"

"Trev, you're going to have to deal with this eventually. Cez is your brother. Marlena's pregnant with your niece. Sooner or later—"

"Niece?"

"Huh?"

"They're having a girl?"

Baz pauses for a second. "Yeah. They announced it tonight. They're expecting a daughter."

If hurting my mother's feelings pinched my heart, this is like a kick with cleats to the gut. My brother and ex-fiancée are having a little girl this spring, and it hurts like fuck, because Marlena and I used to talk about having kids. She always said that if we had a daughter, that little girl would have me wrapped around her pinkie, and I'd nod and tell her that was one hundred percent true. I try to ignore the sudden burst of longing that steals my breath away.

"Trev? You there?"

"Uh…yeah. What are they naming her?"

"Aurora."

I nod, the clenching in my chest easing just a little. At least he didn't say "Camilla," which was the name Marlena and I had picked out for *our* future daughter.

"If they have a second child, they can call it Borealis," I say.

"Dad made that joke too."

Figures. My dad and I have the same sense of humor.

"Come tomorrow," says Baz.

"I am," I tell him. "I'll be over in the morning and stay through dinner."

"Umm…" Baz clears his throat. "Yeah. Okay. Cool, cool, cool."

Fuck. He's not telling me something.

"What?" I ask.

"No, that's great. You're coming tomorrow. Awesome."

"Baz…spit it out. Now."

"Fuck," he mutters. "Fine. They're coming tomorrow too."

"Cez and Marlena? Are you kidding me?"

He sighs softly. "Mom got all blubbery about the baby and asked them what they were doing tomorrow, and they didn't have any plans, so she insisted that they come for the day."

Well, that's that. "Then I guess I won't be there, after all."

"Trevor, please."

"I have to g-go," I say, the words sticking in my throat.

"No! Come! Just come tomorrow. You don't have to talk to them. You can just—"

"I'm going to the Golden Buddha for dinner, Baz. If you want to see me, you can find me there, but I swear to God, if you show up with Cez—"

"I wouldn't do that," he insists.

"Gotta go," I say, because my eyes are burning and I seriously don't feel like dealing with this shit anymore.

"Trev—"

I lean forward and hang up the call, watching as the display changes from "Baz Calling" to "Call Ended."

A moment later, my phone rings again, but I don't pick up. I don't want to talk to my brother again tonight. I don't want to hear about how sorry Cez is or how I need to forgive him or about how Marlena is carrying my parents' first grandchild and that it's been half a year since she broke our engagement and I need to make room in my heart for that baby. I don't want to be guilt-tripped or criticized. I don't want to fight. I just don't want to spend Christmas with my cheating brother and his pregnant fiancée. And if that means I won't see my parents at Christmas this year? So be it.

Forgiveness is a sticky thing, I think, heading north on Route 2 toward home.

Faye offered it so easily tonight, even though I treated her like trash at the bar. But I am totally unable to extend a shred of it to my brother.

I wish I could, I think to myself. I wish I *could* forgive him, because the peace that comes with offering forgiveness is almost as joyful as the relief that comes with being forgiven.

I think of Faye's face as she said "I do." It was free of hurt, free of anger. Perhaps I can't forgive Cez and Marlena yet because I am *still* hurt and *still* angry, and frankly, I don't know when that pain will subside, allowing room for true forgiveness.

But as I get closer and closer to the house that should have been brimming with joy on my first married Christmas, I find that—for the first time since June—my sadness outweighs my anger. For the first time since that terrible night in Portland, I long for the peace and relief that only forgiveness can bring.

***

Faye

I wake up with the sun on Christmas morning…

…at 11:17 a.m. local time.

I do a double-take when I look at the clock radio beside my bed, blinking at the four red digital numbers filling the small screen. I can't remember the last time I woke up this late, especially since my body clock is still probably set to

Boston time, which means I'm actually waking up at 3:17 p.m.!

I chuckle softly as I stretch my arms over my head.

I guess I needed it.

"This is what happens when you don't take a vacation for ten years," I mumble to myself.

Blinking my eyes against the light coming in through my windows, I nestle under the sheets and blanket. For all that the North Pole Inn isn't fancy digs, they make a damn comfortable bed. So comfortable, in fact, I had almost missed the throbbing of my head until now.

"Owww," I whine, closing my eyes and frowning.

How many drinks did I have last night?

I piece together my memories and add them up: a gin martini, several sips of North Star vodka, a tequila shot, and…oh Lord. A scorpion bowl and a half. No wonder I feel like poop. I haven't been hungover in…ages.

Swinging my legs over the bed, I stagger into the bathroom, where I open up my toiletry bag and find some Advil. After swallowing down three tablets chased with a plastic cup of water, I step back to bed, burrowing under the covers and mentally reconstruct the rest of last night.

Thoughts of Brandy-the-bartender make me smile, especially as I recall her perfect martini and confident advice about men. And if memory serves, she invited me to share Christmas dinner with her and everyone else at the Golden Buddha this evening. Though it wouldn't have occurred to me even in my wildest dreams that I'd spend Christmas Day at a strip mall Chinese restaurant surrounded by strangers,

I'm even more surprised by how much I'm looking forward to it.

As my head stops throbbing, I feel a little better and grab my phone off the bedside table. I check my e-mail first and am thankful there are no pressing issues at work. There is, however, a follow-up message from Mr. Fairbanks.

I bite my lower lip in anticipation even as T's face flashes through my brain. Hmm. T, the brokenhearted potato farmer. I hadn't remembered him until now. I don't know when or if I'll ever see T again, but I was certainly attracted to him. I fervently hope that I will be attracted to Mr. Fairbanks too.

Dear Faith:

Merry Christmas if you celebrate. Happy Monday if you don't.

Now that formalities are out of the way and we have an agreement on the table, I wanted to give you the details of our meeting.

I have booked us a suite at the Chalet Blanche, a luxury lodge located just north of Fairbanks, for our weekend together. The chef there will be preparing our meals, so if you have any dietary restrictions, I hope you will feel comfortable sharing them with me in advance so that we may anticipate your needs. Our room will be ready at 3:00 p.m. on Friday. Should you require transportation to and from the airport, please let me know.

In addition to enjoying one another in an intimate fashion, I would also be happy to show you around Fairbanks. The Alaska Railroad is quite scenic, and I would recommend we spend an afternoon at Chena Hot Springs. If you are interested in these attractions, please let me know. I am happy to schedule day trips for our amusement.

Have a wonderful holiday, and see you soon.

Mr. Fairbanks

My toes curl under the covers.

There's something about him that's so confident, so commanding, and yet so mindful of my needs and wishes.

Will he be like that in bed?

My God, I hope so.

A pleasant tremor rocks my body, and I let my phone fall to my chest as I slip my hand into the waistband of my pajama bottoms, smoothing my palm over the flat plane of my stomach and then lower. My middle finger slides between the petals of my folds, and I gasp lightly as its pad touches on the little nub of erect flesh located there.

For all that I am inexperienced with men, I know my body. I know what excites me. I know how to pleasure myself. As I rub my clit, slipping my finger lower to slicken it in my juices, I close my eyes, picturing T's face. I have no idea what Mr. Fairbanks looks like, but I bring myself to orgasm thinking of T's face and hoping that our banter at the bar is the sort of conversation I'll enjoy with my first lover. My hips buck off the bed as I climax, shiver, then sigh, riding out the sweet waves of pleasure before picking up my phone again.

Since I last looked, a red bubble has appeared over my texting app, and I'm pleased to discover it's a message from my sister.

HARRIET: Merry Christmas, Faye! I miss you. Please call today. xo

I type in a quick response.

FAYE: Merry Christmas. I don't want to interrupt your plans, so why don't you call me instead? I am at leisure until this evening. I hope you are enjoying Vail. xo

Not five minutes later, my phone chirps at me, and I slide it off the bedside table to answer.

"Hello?"

"Faye? It's Harry."

"Merry Christmas, Harriet!" I say, sitting up in bed. "How's Vail?"

"Oh, it's…nice."

Her lackluster tone isn't lost on me. "Is anything wrong?"

"No. I just…" She sighs. "How are you?"

I'm about to say "Just fine" when I remember thinking about Harriet last night—specifically, about how stiff and awkward our conversations are and how much I wish they were more fun, more natural.

"Actually? I'm a little hungover."

She gasps loudly. *"What? You are?"*

I allow myself a chuckle. "I am. I had something called a 'scorpion bowl' last night—"

"Were you at a Thai place?"

"Chinese."

"Oh, my God! Faye! I can't even imagine you drunk! How did that *happen*?"

I laugh again. "Well…I was at this Chinese place, and

the bartender asked if I wanted to share dinner during her break. She ordered the scorpion bowl for me to try."

Harriet giggles. "Are you a lightweight?"

I had over forty ounces! "For your information, Harry, I dra—"

"Oh, my God! Faye!"

"What?"

"You just called me 'Harry'!"

"What do you mean?"

"You just said, 'For your information, *Harry*,' not 'For your information, *Harriet*.'"

"Why is this of note?"

"Because you never, ever call me 'Harry.' You're always formal. Always."

"Surely not always…"

"Always," she insists.

My shoulders slump because she's right.

Suddenly, I flash back to my little sister standing beside me at our parents' gravesite. We lingered for a few minutes as extended family, friends, and business associates slipped quietly away. I remember her taking my larger hand in hers and clutching on to it as we stood there side by side. But I also remember pulling my hand away, because I had held it together all day and that one gesture threatened all of my careful composure.

"You know what?" I say gently. "I can try to loosen up."

"Really?"

"Mm-hm."

"So maybe we could drink a scorpion bowl together the next time I visit?"

This is a shocking suggestion because Harriet never initiates visits, only grudgingly agrees to them when I insist. It makes me smile. It may even make my eyes water a little, but then again, we can't lose our minds completely. We are New Englanders, after all.

"When you're twenty-one, yes."

She laughs again, and I find myself smiling even wider, because I haven't enjoyed a conversation with my sister in years…and I'm actually enjoying this one. Very much. And that in itself is a bit of a Christmas miracle.

"Now, you be honest with me, Harry: Did I hear a dip in your voice before? When I asked about Vail?"

"So you know how I'm here with my friend, Jordan? Her brother, Austin, is here too."

"Mm-hm. Yes."

"He's superhot and goes to Dartmouth, and I was, like, *sure* he was into me, but then this other friend of the family came over last night, and he was sort of ignoring me and spending time with her. But now, today, he's back to giving me all this attention, and I'm just not sure…"

"About?"

"If I should…you know, be attracted to him?"

"You either are or you aren't," I say, a flashback of T filling my brain and making me shiver. "Attraction isn't a choice. It's instinctual."

"Okay. I am attracted to him," she says with a sigh. "But I think he might be a player."

"A 'player,'" I say. "Like…someone who plays around?"

"Exactly."

"And you're not sure…"

"You know, whether or not to…go for it. Because he's going to try to kiss me today. I know it. And I want to kiss him back, but if that girl comes over again and he ignores me, I'll just feel…you know, bad."

I suddenly realize that I have absolutely no idea if my sister is still a virgin or if she's far more experienced than I am, but based on this conversation, I think I should probably assume the latter. And yet for all that she's more physically experienced, she's not certain of what she should do in this particular situation. She's been with men, but she's still learning about them.

And for the first time I can ever remember, she's asking *me* for advice.

(When what I know would fill a thimble!)

Luckily, Brandy's words from last night come back to me in a blazing flash of truth, and I have some wisdom to offer my little sister.

"Harry," I say. "Only be with a guy who's crazy about you. Don't settle for less."

She's silent for several seconds, and I finally realize that she's crying. Softly. In hushed sobs and whispered whimpers.

"Oh no. Oh dear. Harry, it's okay. I promise it'll be okay. There are so many other boys out there—"

"Faye," she weeps. "Where…h-have you…b-been?"

The words are broken and stilted over the phone line, and they tug and pull at my heart, making my eyes burn again.

I have been there for her in some ways: ensuring her education and making sure she never wanted for anything material. But emotionally? I've been a terrible guardian and an even more terrible sister. Not because I *meant* to be…but because I allowed other things in my life to take precedence. And I'm sorry for it now. I'm so sorry.

"Harry, we're going to change things, okay? I'm going to…loosen up. And we're going to talk more. Like sisters. I promise."

She sniffles. "I've w-wanted that for so l-long, Faye."

So have I.

The words slide through my head in slow motion, and though I won't burden her with *my* emotional needs, I think I'm finally ready to step up and meet hers.

"Next summer," I say, "when you're home, maybe we could do some traveling together."

"I'd love that!"

"We could go to Scandinavia, and to Germany, of course. Maybe to some of the Eastern European distilleries that are—"

"Wait. What?"

"Yes! There are some real up-and-comers in Poland and the Ukraine, and I think we'd have a marvelous—"

"You're talking about me coming along on a business trip," she says, her voice flatter and softer than it was a moment ago.

"Yes! Of course."

"I thought…" She sighs. "Yeah. Maybe we could do that."

I don't know what just happened. Perhaps my sister doesn't like travel? But she just said she'd love to travel with me. Perhaps she doesn't like distilleries? Or business? But that's impossible. One day we'll run Findley Imports together, won't we?

"I should go," she says. "It's two o'clock here, and I think we're going skiing for a few hours before coming back for dinner."

"Yes, of course," I say. "Mustn't be rude to your hosts."

"Faye," she says softly. "I'm glad you called. I'm going to think about what you said—about only being with a guy who's crazy about me and not settling for less."

"I'm glad, Harry," I say. "I think it's good advice."

"Merry Christmas, Faye," she says. "I…I…" She clears her throat. "I hope you have a wonderful day."

Something's wrong, but I don't know what. I don't know how this conversation went from giggles and advice to her voice being so flat and sad. I wish I knew, but we don't have time to discuss it. Her friends are waiting for her.

"You too, Harry," I say. "Be good. Have fun."

"Good-b-bye," she says, but before I can wish her "Merry Christmas, Harry," my phone sounds in three quick tones to tell me she's already hung up.

CHAPTER SIX

Trevor

Over the past several years while I was dating Marlena, I didn't attend the Golden Buddha Christmas dinner.

She went with me the first year we were dating, but I could tell she was uncomfortable with Ping's excited, broken English and the obscure Chinese food he made to honor the holiday for his American friends. He explained to me that wormwood dumplings, pickled jellyfish, and century eggs are true Chinese delicacies that required him to import special ingredients, but Marlena's Western palate couldn't stomach the strange flavors, and we stopped attending the dinner together after the first year.

Truth be told? Ping's "special" dishes aren't my favorites either, but I know that he's trying to both assimilate and show respect, and so I prepare myself to struggle through the slimy texture of his jellyfish and the cheese-like chewiness of his preserved egg yolks as I walk through the door of the Golden Buddha on Monday afternoon.

The mouth-watering smells of typical Chinese food greet me as I step inside, with Bing Crosby crooning about white Christmases and the hum of cheerful conversation rounding out the festive atmosphere.

Ping and his sons, John and James, have moved all the restaurant's tables into one long banquet table running through the center of the dining room, and more than half of the seats are already filled with restaurant employees and their families and friends. And *on* the table there is an assortment of shared food: a whole roasted turkey, a honey ham, a sweet potato casserole, and several baskets of biscuits and dinner rolls, plus trays of sushi and a full pan of lasagna. Everyone contributes something, and no one goes home hungry.

"T!" yells Ping from the head of the table. "You come to my dinner this year!"

In my arms I'm carrying a case of North Star vodka, and I offer it to him with a wide grin. "It's been too long, Ping! I missed it."

"Merry Christmas!" he booms in his heavy accent, telling his son in Mandarin to take the case of liquor to the bar.

Someone pinches my arm, and I turn to see Brandy standing beside me. "Hey, stranger."

"Hey."

"You get Faye home safely last night?" she asks me.

"Sure did."

She nods with approval. "What're you drinking? I'll grab you something."

As she heads off to the bar to pour me a pint of hard cider, I take an empty seat near the center of the table, looking up as the bell over the front door jingles. Dressed in jeans and a fur-trimmed parka I see Faye, standing uncertainly in the doorway.

I stand up and slide through the crowd to welcome her, grinning at her pink cheeks and hesitant expression.

"Hi," I say. "Remember me?"

"Of course." Her blush deepens. "Merry Christmas, T."

"Merry Christmas, Faye."

She unbuttons her coat, and I take it from her, hanging it up on the stand behind me. Wearing a black turtleneck sweater with pearls, she looks chic and classy.

"How's your head?" I ask.

She shrugs. "Thank God for Advil. Plus, I have it on good authority that I got most of the poison out last night."

"Yes," I tell her, chuckling softly. "I was an eyewitness to the purge."

She cringes. "Sorry."

"Nuh-uh. You don't have to apologize for that."

As we approach the table together, she places a hand on my arm. "Wait! Is this a potluck? Oh God. I didn't bring anything!"

"I brought a case of vodka," I tell her. "We can just say it was from both of us."

"Thanks," she says, her dark eyes sparkling as she smiles at me.

"It's the least I can do," I tell her, pulling out the chair beside mine and sitting down next to her.

"Faye!" Brandy appears behind us, holding out my cider, and Faye stands up to hug her. "Brandy, thank you so much for inviting me!"

"I'm glad you came. What are you drinking? I have a

very decent prosecco open."

"Sounds divine," says Faye.

"I'll grab you one, and when I come back, I'll introduce you to everyone, okay?" Brandy turns to me. "Behave yourself."

I hold up three fingers in a Scout's oath. "Promise."

Faye sits back down, then turns to me. "Speaking of introductions, we didn't really meet properly yesterday. I'm Faye Findley."

Faye...Findley. I *know* that name. How do I know that name? I stare at her, trying to figure out where we've met, but I can't place her.

"Your name is so familiar," I tell her.

"Really?"

Faye Findley. Faye Findley.

I nod. "What do you do?"

"I own a company back east called Findley Imports that—"

"Of course!" I exclaim. "Findley Imports! You're trying to buy my business!"

She leans back, shaking her head, her expression perplexed. "A...potato farm? No. I think you're mistaken—"

"The farm is my *family's* business," I tell her. "*I* started North Star Spirits with my brothers five years ago!"

Her lips part, her mouth opening to a perfect O as she stares at me. "You're...Trevor Starling? *T* is for Trevor?"

"*T* is for Trevor." I nod, holding out my hand. "It's good to meet you, Faye Findley."

"Holy sh—I mean, my goodness! I had no idea…I—" Suddenly she laughs. "No wonder North Star vodka is your favorite!"

"And yours," I remind her. "No wonder you know so much about liquor!"

She's probably one of the foremost authorities in the country. Her company is one of the largest importers and distributors in the nation.

"Your product is delicious. I wasn't sucking up."

"I believe you. It's damn good vodka," I tease, then shake my head, marveling at this turn of events. "Last night you said you came to Alaska to meet with the owner of a company you want to acquire."

She nods. "That's right."

"So you're actually up here to meet…me."

"Yes." She laughs softly. "I am."

Now this is intriguing. This woman flew all the way from the East Coast to spend Christmas in North Pole, Alaska, hoping to check out my operation and meet *me*. It's certainly flattering.

But it's also daunting. Especially because I'm not interested in selling my company. I never have been. I'm possessive of what's mine, and that includes North Star Spirits. That said, however, I can't resist the urge to show it off either.

"Are you free tomorrow?" I ask her. "I can show you the distillery operations if you're interested."

"There's nothing I'd like better," she says.

"But I warn you," I follow up quickly, "this company is

my baby. I'm not going to sell."

Her smile is enigmatic. "I've heard that before."

"I'm not selling." I lift my chin and add some steel to my voice. "I won't."

"Okay."

"You don't believe me."

"I didn't say that."

I lean forward, close enough to smell her perfume, which is subtle and clean and messes with my head a little. "It's not going to happen."

That slight, secretive smile stays securely in place as she nods her head once. "Understood."

Her one-word answers are maddening because I can't help feeling that she has some ironclad agenda that will somehow undermine my current determination. It's unsettling.

"Prosecco for you," says Brandy, returning with a full flute of bubbles. "Come and meet my mom and dad, Faye."

I watch Faye move around the room, admiring her as she accepts hugs from strangers with grace and warmth. But I'm downright astonished when Brandy introduces her to Ping, and she greets him in Mandarin and wishes him, I assume, a Merry Christmas.

"Wow! Wow! Wow! An English lady who speak Chinese!" he exclaims in English, clasping her hands in his. "Miss Faye, you are most welcome!"

"*Syeh-syeh, Ping sheng*," she says with a small bow. "I am so grateful for your kindness and hospitality."

By the time she returns to my side and sits down, her

glass is empty, and Brandy takes it back to the bar to fill it up.

"Nicely done," I tell her. "You're a hit."

"I travel a great deal," she tells me, reaching for a plate of dumplings and putting one on her plate. "It always helps to be able to say 'thank you' and 'please' in the language of my host."

"So…do you actually know Chinese?"

"Not at all." She shakes her head. "I just learned a few phrases for tonight."

"That was thoughtful. How?"

"The internet," she says with a little shrug.

"You're industrious."

She grins as she takes a bite of the dumpling.

"But I'm still not selling, Faye."

"We'll see."

***

My brother texts me that he's too tired to drive down to North Pole after spending the day at my parent's house and that he'll see me in the office at some point tomorrow.

Although I love Baz, I'm relieved he's not coming. I've been enjoying myself, sandwiched between some guys from the North Pole fire department and Faye Findley.

I barely know her, of course, but there's something about meeting her last night and sitting next to her today that makes me feel connected to her. Like…I don't know— she's not my date or anything, obviously, but I wouldn't mind if she were. It's a shallow but delightful feeling, likely fueled more by cider and Christmas than any actual sentiments I have for her.

All I know is that seeing my brother would shatter the illusion that I'm just a normal single guy spending Christmas with a roomful of friends, with the good fortune of being seated beside a smart, beautiful woman.

Several hours later, as the evening winds down and guests take turns loading dishes and platters in Ping's industrial dishwasher and wrapping up leftovers to take home, I nudge Faye with my elbow.

"Need an escort back to your digs?"

She starts to yawn, then covers her mouth quickly and laughs. "Sure. Thanks."

We say goodnight to Ping and his family; Denny, Brandy, and their folks; the guys from the fire department and ambulance corps who came by for leftovers; and other friends who stopped in for a glass of Christmas cheer. I help her with her coat and hold the door open as we step outside into the cold.

"Wow, it's chilly!" she exclaims, zipping up her parka and pulling mittens out of her pockets.

"Welcome to Alaska in December," I tell her.

"Thank you," she says, with a light chuckle. "But you know what? It's no worse than New York City the day before yesterday, actually."

"No way that's true."

"It is!" she insists. "The way the wind whistles down the streets and avenues? It's freezing. Have you ever visited?"

"To New York?" I shake my head. "Nope. Chicago is

the closest I've ever been."

"You're missing out," she tells me. "There's nowhere in the world like New York."

"Then I'll have to add it to my agenda."

"If we go into business together," she says, "you'll have a good reason to come east, *and* you'll be able to write it off."

"Business *together*?" I ask. "Your acquisitions guy—"

"Karl Franklin," she supplies.

"Yeah. Karl. He never said anything about working *together*. Only about you buying us out."

She takes a deep breath. "There's always room for negotiation."

With everything? I wonder. *Would anything have made a difference yesterday? Would anything have enticed you into my bed?*

I instantly grimace at the direction of my thoughts for two reasons:

1. Because now that I know Faye is Faye *Findley*, she's a business associate, and I don't shit where I eat. I would never get involved romantically with someone who could directly affect the success of North Star. And…

2. Because when I got home last night, the first thing I did was write a message to Faith Crawford about her upcoming trip to Fairbanks. Though Faith and I have no commitment to one another aside from spending New Year's weekend together, it would weirdly feel like cheating to get involved with Faye in the interim…or with Faith directly after. I paint a wide line now when it comes to cheating, and even though I *technically* wouldn't be cheating on anyone, it just doesn't feel right.

In fact, as attracted as I am to Faye, I'm relieved that she turned me down yesterday. I enjoy her—that's for sure—and I've noticed that I haven't been brooding as much since meeting her yesterday, but we can't have a romantic future if we're business associates. I won't let it happen, and I'd be willing to wager, neither would she.

"I'm looking forward to seeing your distillery tomorrow," she says.

"The distillery you will never own," I say, baiting her for a snappy comeback.

"I already own so many," she says airily. "What's one more?"

"Or less?"

She laughs. "You're tenacious."

"I could say the same about you."

"I just know what I want," she tells me.

And *fuck* but her words—which I'm sure aren't meant to be sexy—affect me like an aphrodisiac. There's something about her that's both sweetly innocent and insanely arousing. I'm fairly certain that no one in the world banters like Faye Findley. No one. It's an art form with this woman.

No wonder she owns so many distilleries. I bet a lot of her negotiations start with a no, and then somehow, before the poor bastard can figure out how the hell it happened, he's signed on the dotted line, ready to sell his soul to her. She's good at what she does…not that that was ever in question. Findley Imports didn't become the company it is today because its leader is feckless.

We get back to her hotel way too soon for my taste and

stop in front of the entrance, facing each other.

"Well," she says, "this is me...for tonight, at least."

My heart clutches. "Are you leaving soon?"

"I'm moving to a place called the Chalet Blanche tomorrow," she tells me. "I did some research, and I think it's a little more my style."

I try to keep my face impassive, but I don't know if I succeed.

The Chalet Blanche is where Faith Crawford and I will be trysting this weekend, and I'm suddenly, *incredibly* uncomfortable about these two parts of my life possibly colliding. My whole point in arranging to meet Faith was to have a discreet affair with a beautiful woman at a posh resort where I'd know no one. It'll hardly be discreet if my lover and I are sharing the four-room, extremely intimate boutique hotel with Faye Findley, with whom I may be doing a business deal. There's no doubt we'd run into one another...at the hotel restaurant or lobby bar or spa. My God, our rooms could technically share a wall. My mind whirls, and my stomach flips over.

"Hey. Are you okay?" Faye asks me, placing a mittened hand on my arm.

"How long are you staying there?"

"A few days," she says, sliding her hand from my arm. "Do you know it? The Chalet Blanche?"

I nod, feeling discombobulated. "Yes. It's...mostly for tourists, of course, but yes. I know it. It's very nice."

"Oh. Good." She glances over her shoulder. "No offense to the North Pole Inn, but I'm tired of being referred to as 'Faye Kringle,' and I'm definitely looking forward to the spa at the Chalet Blanche. I read that it's very intimate."

Shit. This isn't good. *Shit. Shit. Shit.*

Maybe I should rebook Faith and myself to another hotel? But there's no other place in Fairbanks that comes close to the Chalet. It's the only five-star lodging in the area, and I promised Faith Crawford a luxury weekend. I think of her standing on that sailboat, wearing Chanel sunglasses and a Longines diamond watch. I can't take a woman like that to the Hampton Inn.

Faye is still grinning at me, no doubt thinking about high-end spa treatments.

I wish I could circle back to how long she's staying at the Chalet Blanche, but I can't think of a noncreepy way to ask her if she'll be gone by Friday, so I leave the whole thing alone. She *can't* be staying for another week, right? Her whole point in coming up here was to take a peek at my business and make me an offer.

Aha! That's it!

As soon as our business is finished, she'll be headed back to New York. Which means that the length of her visit is completely under my control. That's comforting…and makes me want to get down to business as soon as possible.

"So…how about I pick you up at nine o'clock tomorrow morning?"

"Works for me."

"I'll give you a tour of Starling Farms, where we grow the potatoes we use in North Star vodka, and then take you to the distillery and tasting room."

"Perfect."

Without warning, she rises up on tiptoes and quickly presses her lips to each of my cheeks in a gesture that throws me completely off-balance. Yes, I understand it's an acceptable farewell in Europe, but we're not *in* Europe. We're in North Pole, Alaska, and no one does that.

"Merry Christmas, Trevor Starling," she says softly, that mysterious little smile back in place.

Before I can find my voice, and with the echo of her lips still brushing my skin, she's back inside her hotel, leaving me peering through the glass once again like a lost little boy who has no idea how he got there.

***

Faye

I'm waiting in the hotel lobby with a cup of coffee when Trevor Starling pulls up in a shiny black Jeep Grand Cherokee, puts it in park, hops out of the driver's side, and has the passenger door open before I step off the curb.

"Good morning!" he says.

"Hi!"

"Want me to hold your coffee?"

I hand it to him, climb into the butter-leather tan passenger seat and fasten my seat belt. He hands me my coffee, slams my door closed, and circles the car.

"Cold out this morning," he says, rubbing his hands together.

"Twelve degrees," I lament.

"*Now* tell me that New York is just as cold as Alaska."

I take my phone out of my purse and check the weather in New York. "Nope. It's a balmy thirty-six there."

"Are you warm enough?" he asks, reaching for the climate knob on the console.

"Yes. It's toasty in here."

"Then we're off," he says, grinning at me as he pulls out from under the porte cochere and onto the road in back of the hotel. "Bright sun, though. A nice clear day for you to check out everything."

I glance over at him and quickly assess that he is, without question, the best-looking man of my acquaintance. His thick dark hair is slicked back and his mint-colored eyes outshine the morning sun. Though I've met Trevor twice now, and both times I would have called him handsome, he looks especially delicious this morning: freshly shaven, freshly showered, and brimming with vim and vigor.

"Something tells me you're a morning person, Trevor."

"Yes I am, Faye." He glances at me. "Are you?"

"Naturally? No. Out of necessity? Yes."

"How often do you allow yourself to sleep in?"

"Oh…" I shrug. The truth is that Christmas morning was the first time in years that I've slept in. "Not often. Every now and then."

"I can't imagine it's easy, what you do. Managing one of the largest liquor importation and distribution companies in the country."

"I surround myself with good people," I tell him. "But yes. The buck stops with me." For no good reason I can fathom, I add, "I lost my parents when I was young. Just out of undergrad. I…well, I guess I wanted to make them proud."

"Your father started Findley Imports?"

"Yes. With my grandfather."

"But you kept it going."

Hmm. "Why do I feel like I'm being interviewed?"

"I spent some time online last night looking into you."

"Fair enough. Due diligence?"

"No," he says. "I'd only do due diligence if I were going to sell to you…which I'm not."

I can't help chuckling because this is becoming a familiar theme between us. "Then…?"

"Curiosity."

"And what did you find out?"

"Let's see. You were the adult heir to your father and grandfather's company and fortune, but you have a younger sibling."

"Mm-hm. My sister, Harry."

"Harry? Your sister's name is Harry?"

"No. Her nickname is Harry. Her name is Harriet."

"Ah. Right. Hmm. Let's see. You went to Cornell University in New York."

"True."

"You were born in Boston."

"Yes."

"But you don't still live there."

"No," I say. "I moved out of the city some time ago."

"I see. And, um, well, you've tripled the size and profitability of Findley Imports since taking the helm."

"Also accurate."

"You are unmarried, and according to Wikipedia, you are not involved with anyone. Romantically."

Inside, I bristle a little at this. It's true, of course, but it embarrasses me too, which puts me on the defensive. How exactly was I supposed to triple the size and profitability of my family's company while also nurturing a healthy relationship?

Trevor must sense my discomfort. He clears his throat. "Sorry."

"No," I say. "No. It's fine." I smooth my tan wool slacks and fold my hands on my lap. "It's not untrue. I haven't"—I clear my throat—"dated much."

"Shit," mutters Trevor. "Insert-foot-in-mouth disease. Some days I've got it bad."

I shrug. "Like I said, it's not untrue."

"I'm sure you've had plenty of romances," says Trevor.

I turn my head to look at him. "Are you?"

"Um...well, yes. You're young and pretty. Incredibly successful. You're probably just very discreet."

It feels good when he calls me "pretty," but his use of the word "discreet" makes me think about Mr. Fairbanks' ad and my impending affair, which—for no good reason—dims the brightness of his compliment.

"Yes. I know how to be discreet...but honestly, I haven't had many romances." I have no idea why I'm telling him this. It's really not an appropriate conversation to have with a possible business partner, but Trevor Starling and I have had quite a few inappropriate conversations at this point. How can another hurt? "My life has been consumed by work since my parents passed away. Well, that and...I think I'm a late bloomer."

"A 'late bloomer'? What does that mean?"

"I haven't had *any*," I murmur. "Romances."

I'd imagined the words being spoken in my head. It's with a bit of horror that I realize I've said them aloud.

"*What?* What do you mean?"

I look up at him. "N-Nothing."

"When was your last relationship?" he asks me.

"Well...I have many relationships. My sister. My employees. Friends—"

"With a man."

Never. "It's, um...been a while."

We're stopped at a red light as we approach Fairbanks, and Trevor turns to me, his wide, minty eyes scanning my face. His lips part in surprise as my cheeks flush with heat, and I turn away from him, looking out the window.

"Are we—ahem—almost in, um, Fairbanks?"

He doesn't answer, but I can feel him staring at me. Like I'm a freak.

My breathing speeds up, and my cheeks are almost unbearably warm, but I don't look at him. We're perilously close to him asking if I've *ever* had a boyfriend, which I haven't. I stare out the window, willing him not to say something that will make me want to die on the spot.

"You've given up a lot," he whispers in a rush.

I snap my neck to the left and face him. "Don't feel sorry for me."

"I don't," he says evenly, turning back to look out the windshield. "But aren't you lonely?"

"No," I say quickly. But, fuck, of course I'm lonely, and Trevor Starling and I seem to have a knack for engaging in inappropriate subjects, and somehow it's making things not more uncomfortable between us but less. Somehow, against all odds, our strange experiences—his proposition and my vomit and our realization that we're in the same business and sharing Christmas Eve and Christmas dinner together as virtual strangers—have drawn us closer together, have created an intimacy between us that I find I...*like*. "Yes, I am. Sometimes I'm very lonely."

"What are you going to do about that, Faye Findley?"

Something about the way he asks this question—it could be the way he words it like a challenge or the teasing tone of his voice—makes me smile from ear to ear. And my plan to meet Mr. Fairbanks doesn't feel quite a tawdry as it did a moment ago.

"I'm working on it, Trevor Starling."

"Well, I won't bet against you," he tells me, turning off the main road and into a driveway with a large sign overhead that reads, "Starling Farms." "That's for sure."

CHAPTER SEVEN

Trevor

My parents, Barbara Gibbons and Linus Schwartz, were hippies who met on a commune in Idaho in the late 1970s, married in 1982, legally changed their surname to "Starling," and moved to Alaska, sight unseen, in 1983 with the wackadoodle idea to buy a parcel of land in Fairbanks and start the northernmost potato farm in the United States.

Somehow, their plan went off without a hitch, and by 1995, they had three sons to add to the mix: Trevor, Basil, and Cecil, all named for my British mother's quirky uncles, who are still alive and kicking back in England.

As we pull up in front of their sprawling log cabin house that's been added on to more times than I can count, I cut the engine and turn to Faye.

"My parents are...characters."

"I like characters."

"They met on a commune."

"How unique."

"My mom's British."

"One of my favorite countries."

"Are you fazed by anything?"

"I try not to be, especially when it comes to business."

"I'm not selling," I tell her.

"I know," she answers, smiling at me.

"Infuriating," I sigh.

"I agree," she says, which makes me shake my head and grin.

"Indefatigable."

"Surrender is not an option," she says in a passable English accent, unbuckling her seat belt and opening her car door.

For years and years, my parents worked the farm mostly on their own, but now they hire a staff of six year-round employees and more during the harvest. During the wintertime, when the fields are blanketed in white, the farm itself is quiet except for the massive, bubble-covered plot of year-round earth that's mostly tended by their employees.

My parents aren't expecting us today—I didn't return my mother's calls on Christmas Eve or Day, feeling a measure of betrayal for the way they welcomed Cez and Marlena to the farm both days—but I have brought their Christmas gifts. I pop open the trunk, and Faye joins me, peeking inside.

"Can I help?"

I hand her two wrapped boxes. "Sure."

Cradling another four boxes in my arms, I manage to elbow the button that closes the trunk and lead the way to the front porch. I knock on the door, and after a moment, my father opens it.

"Trevor!" he exclaims, his smile wide under a bushy snow-white beard. "Barb, Trev's here!" His eyes slip to Faye.

"And he brought a girl!"

I take a deep breath and roll my eyes. I love my father, but he is endlessly embarrassing. "Dad, this is Faye Findley, a business associate."

"She's not his girlfriend!" he bellows. "She's a business—"

"Linus, I'm here. Stop yelling, love."

"—associate," he finishes.

"Hello darling," says my mother, dressed in jeans and a South American–style woolen poncho. Her gray hair is wiry and wild, and she wears Birkenstock sandals with colorful striped socks that read "Love is love" in a repeat pattern. "Come in, come in. We missed you yesterday, Trevor."

For all that my parents are hippies-turned-farmers, my mother is still a mother, and there's an undertone of disappointment in her voice that makes me feel guilty.

But no. Just no. Screw that.

"You know why I wasn't here, Mom," I say, following my parents down four steps and into a sunken living room dominated by a massive flagstone fireplace with a roaring fire.

The heart of my childhood house, it's a comfortable room with floor-to-ceiling windows that look out over the farm, Indian rugs, overstuffed sofas that have seen better days, and the open newspapers that my parents were probably reading before we arrived. It's lived-in and welcoming, and my parents' very evil cat, Spud, stretches his legs on the coffee table, eyeing me and Faye lazily before closing his eyes again.

"Spud's still alive, huh?"

My mother races to her "other baby" and perches on the edge of the coffee table beside him. "Spud still has a lot of good years left."

I place the gifts on the couch across from my mother, and Faye does the same. She's been hovering behind me since we arrived, but now my mother's piercing green eyes slide to her. "Hi."

"Hello," says Faye, stepping forward to offer my mother her hand.

"You are…?"

"Mom, this is Faye Findley. She owns the largest beverage importation company in North America."

My mother's eyes narrow just a touch as she holds out her hand. "Barbara Starling."

Faye takes her hand and shakes it. "Nice to meet you, Barbara."

"Nice to meet you, Faye," she answers. "Here on business?"

"Yes," says Faye. "I'm buying Trevor's company."

"I hadn't realized it was for sale."

"It's not," I say.

Faye looks over her shoulder at me and smiles.

"I see," says my mother, and when I slide my eyes from Faye to her, I find that my mother's expression has changed entirely. Her eyes sparkle, and her lips tilt up in a small smile as she eyes Faye with interest. Suddenly, she tilts her head to the side. "Marlena was here yesterday."

I sigh, shoving my hands in my pockets. "I heard."

"They're having a little girl," she shares.

"Heard that too."

"How lovely for you," says Faye, stepping back so that her shoulder brushes against my arm and she is standing directly beside me. "Your first grandchild."

My mother's chin lifts just a touch as she looks at Faye, then at me, then at Faye. "Yes. We're very excited."

"I'm sure," says Faye, the back of her hand grazing the back of mine.

I know what she's doing, and I'm so touched by her solidarity, so surprised by her quiet support that, for the first time in months, the sting of Marlena's pregnancy doesn't steal my breath away. I don't want to scream or cry or thrash at the heavens, railing on about her betrayal. I can stomach it. I can bear it. And the relief I feel is…extraordinary.

"Marlena's, um…healthy?" I ask.

My mother's eyes widen in surprise. "She is. She and the baby are both well."

I nod once. That's about all the polite conversation I can handle for now, so I turn to my father. "Do any hunting yesterday, Dad?"

"Yep. Baz came along with me for a while."

"Get anything?"

"Got a deer draining in the game shed."

"Good for you."

"We missed you, son."

"Ping did his regular Christmas dinner. Faye came along."

My father looks at Faye, offering his hand to her. "I'm

Linus, Faye. Trev's old dad."

She reaches out her hand. "Nice to meet you, Linus."

"How long are you in town?"

"A few days," she answers.

I realize that this is the standard answer she's given several times now, and I wonder if she has a return ticket or not. Perhaps she hasn't even booked a flight home yet. What surprises me is the short, quick flash of melancholy I feel thinking about her departure. Last night, I realized I needed to hasten it if I wanted her gone before Faith Crawford arrives, but right now? Standing here in my parent's living room beside her? I hate the idea of her leaving.

"Trevor's showing me the distillery today, but I understand he uses potatoes grown here on your farm? For his vodka?"

"Have you tasted it?" asks my dad, his voice brimming with pride.

Faye chuckles. "Actually, Linus, it's my favorite. I think it's the best vodka on the market today."

My father nods in appreciation, pointing a calloused, stubby finger at the woman standing beside me. "I *like* you, Faye Findley!"

My mother nods in agreement as she looks on, stroking Spud's soft calico coat.

Me too, I think, glancing down at her in time to catch her deep brown eyes look up to grab mine. *I like her too.*

***

My father gives us a short tour of the all-season garden, which is protected and climate-controlled, and my mother thanks us for visiting before we get in the car for the drive over to the North Star offices, distillery, and tasting room.

"My parents liked you," I tell her as we pull out of their driveway.

"I liked them too," she says, "though I'm sorry you didn't get to spend Christmas with them."

"That was my choice," I say. "I was welcome to join them, but I wasn't...ready yet."

"That's understandable. I'm sure you're still hurt."

I take a deep breath and sigh. "Believe it or not, I'm less hurt by Marlena than by Cez. I mean, don't get me wrong, it hurt like hell that my fiancée cheated on me with my brother, but it hurt a lot more that my brother would do that to me."

"I get that."

"She wasn't my family, you know? She was *almost* my family. He *was* my family."

"Technically, he still *is*," she says softly.

I bristle against her words. "Family shouldn't act like that."

"And parents shouldn't die in plane crashes. But shit happens."

Surprised by the bluntness of her words, I glance over at her to find her face mostly peaceful. No tears. No self-pity. She's stating facts, I think, not looking for sympathy.

"I'm sorry about that," I tell her. "About your parents."

"Me too." She pauses for a moment, then adds, "Do you know what I'd give for another day, another *hour*, with them?" Her voice is more emotional now. "I think I'd give a decade of my life for a little more time."

"You must have loved them very much."

"They weren't perfect," she says, "but yes, they were everything to me." After a few minutes of silence, she says, "You still have your brother. I know he betrayed you. I know he hurt you. But…"

"But what? Mend things? Forgive him?"

"Yes."

"Believe it or not, I wish I could."

"You can."

"I can't." I shake my head. "I don't trust him."

"You have a lifetime to rebuild trust, but you can't start rebuilding it if you refuse to be around him." She pauses. "I'm not a perfect sister. I recently realized that I've been stingy with her. Keeping her safe and clothed and fed isn't enough. She needs…love. She needs friendship. She needs family. And I'm all she has. If something happened to her? And took away the chance for me to do better? To show her how much I love her? I'd be devastated." She takes a deep breath before continuing, and I sense she's thinking about the loss of her parents, and I'm wondering if there was "unfinished business" between them that still weighs heavy on her heart. "I don't know how yet, but I'm committed to doing better with Harry. Maybe we can spend more time together, have more fun together, build a friendship, be the sort of sisters who share things and support one another. I can love her better. I *know* I can do better."

The unspoken final sentence in her monologue is,

And so can you.

I hear the words in my head as we drive along in

silence, the hum of the car's engine filling the void.

But our circumstances are so different! my mind insists.

Her sister didn't betray her.

Her sister didn't sleep with her fiancé and get pregnant, starting a whole new life on the scorched earth of Faye's torched dreams.

"I'm not sure you can compare our situations," I say.

"Some people would retreat here," she says. "They'd apologize for sharing their opinion so freely, and tell you that you should do what feels right."

"Why do I get the feeling you're not going to do that?"

"Because I'm not." She gives me a grim smile. "There are different types of loss, and you've experienced one that's pretty terrible. But yours—whether you choose to acknowledge it or not—is still fluid. Mine is…irreversible. Unalterable. Set in stone."

"That's true, but—"

"You have both of your parents *and* both of your brothers still alive."

"And I'm furious at one of them."

"T, you have to make your own choices of course, but maybe—just maybe—you've been so consumed with anger that you haven't looked at the situation from every angle," she suggests. "Think of it like a flowchart. Is there any outcome wherein Cez and Marlena's union is a 'best case scenario' for you?"

I think about this for a moment, and I'm surprised by Baz's words from two weeks ago suddenly echoing in my head:

Are you sure you and Marlena had the healthiest relationship?

At the time, I didn't answer his question. I was too angry to consider it. But now I find myself thinking back to my three years with Marlena, and no, I'm not certain we had the healthiest relationship.

Frankly, I'm not certain whatsoever.

Marlena was constantly on my back about the hours I spent at work and was unsupportive of my ambition, even as she cheerfully spent my money.

She worked at the hospital, yes, but she never took extra shifts or spoke about wanting to do or be more. She wasn't passionate about her profession—it was a job, not a career—which probably made it difficult for her to understand my quasi-obsession with building North Star.

And when she wasn't at the hospital, she didn't necessarily want to spend time with me; she liked having "girl time" with her friends, which included manicures, pedicures, chick flicks, and wine.

I would've watched a movie with her now and then, but our preferences were so different. I would choose a documentary or drama that would have her asleep in minutes, while she would choose something silly and shallow that had me rolling my eyes internally.

And while I would have appreciated a companion for hiking, camping, and fishing trips in the summertime, she wasn't interested in spending time outdoors. She was a self-professed "homebody," though from what I recall, that didn't include cooking or cleaning or *keeping* a home. It mostly just seemed to include watching TV, taking long baths, and ordering takeout in said "home."

The sex was good, I think.

But...*was it?*

It was in the beginning.

But as the years rolled on, she wasn't as interested. I was always up for it, and she generally wasn't. It always seemed like she had her period or a headache or had a troubling shift at work that she needed to "process" or that she wanted to "watch TV in peace."

Toward the end, when sex was off the table, I would have been happy just to cuddle with her on the sofa and watch the northern lights, but she thought that was "boring."

Maybe—though it didn't occur to me at the time and stings to admit now—it was *me* she found boring. And maybe, though it would have brought our entire relationship crumbling down around us, I found her boring too. And a little shallow. And superficial. And lazy. And—

Is there any outcome wherein Cez and Marlena's union is a "best case scenario" for you?

"Maybe," I whisper, more to myself than to Faye.

I pull into the parking area in front of my distillery and park in my reserved parking space.

Maybe.

***

Faye

There is something about the shiny metal boilers, mashes, columns, and stills in any distillery operation that feels exciting to me. Almost...*arousing.*

Weird? Maybe.

But I don't care. I can't help it.

Of note, Trevor Starling's hardware is unbelievably gorgeous.

He opted for two 250-gallon copper batch still systems with twelve-inch stainless steel stripping stills and continuous vodka columns.

As I walk into the distilling room, I—*literally*—sigh in pleasure at the sight.

"Ohhh…wow," I breathe.

"You like?" he asks, his smile so insanely and unfairly beautiful beside a shiny copper still, I can't decide where to focus my attention.

"I…*love*," I say softly.

From the outside, the distillery looks rustic—like an old farmer's barn taken over by a hipper, newer business…which is one hundred percent accurate. From the compass painted in metallic silver-blue on the concrete floor to the bottling machine in the far corner, this place is both old-fashioned and high end.

And if I'm being honest, it's my idea of heaven.

"I'm sure you've seen a million distilleries around the world," he says, and I might be wrong, but I think he's angling for a compliment, which I'm happy to give.

"I visited Tito's in Austin recently, and don't get me wrong—I *love* their product, but what they lack in visual aesthetics is everything you've captured here."

"They're hardly 'handcrafted' anymore," he points out. "Do they still have that little pot still at the original distillery site?"

"They do. With a tasting room. That's the one I'm talking about. It lacks the charm of yours."

"Did you visit the facility they opened in 2007? The one with ten stills that makes almost four million cases a year now?"

"Yes, I've visited it. But I'd never compare it to yours. That's a factory. You own a craft distillery."

"Was it pretty cool, though?"

"For what it is, sure." I look around at his modest operation. "Do you aspire to that sort of growth?"

"Not even close," he tells me. "But there's a place in Massachusetts called Berkshire Mountain Distillers, and I'm keen to be on par with them someday. I'd like to do with North Star vodka what they've done with Ethereal gin."

I know the owners of Berkshire very well and have great respect for their product and the way they run their business. It's yet another sign of Trevor's excellent business sense that he'd like to emulate their success.

"They're in nineteen states now," I say.

"Of course you know that," he says, shaking his head lightly as he grins at me. "You're...amazing, Faye."

I feel the blush heat my cheeks, but I don't look away from him. "So are you."

The way he's looking at me, with a fierce focus and intensity, makes my heart beat faster, and I realize that my attraction to him, combined with the kismet of our similar interests, is causing me to...to...*what?* Develop a crush on him? Start having *feelings* for him?

He takes a step forward, his tongue darting out to slicken his lips as he continues to stare at me, and I feel it in my gut and in my hot, sluicing blood: a dizzy sensation—like spinning or falling, but without moving. It's all happening on the inside of me, and it's...*divine*.

Kiss me.

My eyes flick to his lips, and I step closer to him.

Kiss me, Trevor. Please.

My breathing is shallow and erratic, making my chest puff and fall quickly. My pulse races, and my heart thunders in my ears. I lean my head back, my eyes still laser-locked on his.

"Trevor," I whisper. "T."

He freezes, blinking at me. "Faye, I..."

"It's okay," I tell him, my voice low and breathy, my face still upturned toward his.

"No. It's...um...I...I can't." He clenches his jaw, and his eyebrows furrow.

"O-Oh." *My God, was I practically begging him to kiss me! A potential business partner! Have you lost your mind, Faye?* I take a step back, shaking my head in embarrassment. "I'm sorry."

"You didn't do anything wrong," he says. His eyes are darker now, dilated, wide, and troubled. "The timing's just..."

"No need to explain." I clear my throat. "It's for the best."

"Is it?"

"Yes. I'm still hoping to acquire you." Heat flares behind his eyes, and I realize the unintentional double entendre in my words. "No, no! Not *you*. I—I mean…your *company*."

His shoulders relax, and he tilts his head to the side, giving me a small, teasing smile. "That's too bad."

"Why? Because I won't end up acquiring either?" I tease back.

"You never know, Faye." He searches my face, his gaze intense for a moment before he gestures to a set of stairs. "You haven't seen the tasting room yet."

"Lead on."

As I follow him out of the distillery and into the adjacent tasting room, I try to figure out what just happened between us. I know I'm not the most experienced woman, but I am ninety-nine percent certain he was about to kiss me and then he…didn't. And when he didn't, he said, "I can't."

Why? I wonder.

The timing, he'd said.

But why is the *timing* bad? Because we may go into business together someday? Or because he's not over Marlena's betrayal yet? Or perhaps because there's someone else in the picture?

There's someone else in your *picture too*, my brain points out, reminding me of Mr. Fairbanks.

Something inside of me twists painfully when I think of my New Year's date. To give myself so willfully, so intimately, to a man about whom I feel nothing…am I *really* okay with that decision? Because right this second, and for the first time since I answered his ad, it doesn't *feel* okay.

I want to lose my virginity. I do. And losing it to Mr.

Fairbanks, when I had no other prospects on the horizon, felt like a good solution. But now that I've met Trevor? I don't know. It just *doesn't* feel like such a great solution anymore.

Maybe I've made a mistake in minimizing the importance of feelings in this equation.

Maybe it doesn't matter how old you are when you lose your virginity; maybe it shouldn't be lost to someone about whom you feel nothing.

But most of all, I think I've been very wrong to treat the loss of my virginity like a transaction, rather than a once-in-a-lifetime event that's irrevocably bound to my heart…whether I like it or not.

Trevor holds the door to the tasting room open for me, and as I pass him, I inhale his clean, masculine scent. It sends a tremor of longing from my brain to my belly, pooling there, creating these breathtaking flutters of want, of lust, of desire.

Crap. Oh crap, crap, crap.

I wish I had someone to talk to—a wise girlfriend or an older sister who could guide me through these new and confusing feelings. But the absurdity of a thirty-year-old woman being unable to navigate attraction and arousal isn't lost on me either. There *isn't* anyone to talk to. I need to figure this out for myself.

"I assume you'd like to do a tasting?" Trevor asks me.

"Oh! Um, yes. I'd love to."

He gestures to the open stools at the bar as he steps behind it. "Take a seat and I'll get you started."

Pushing my bewildering thoughts and feelings to the side for the time being, I sit down and look up at him expectantly.

"Listen…I'm sorry about before," he says, placing a shot glass in front of me. "Especially after the asinine way I behaved on Christmas Eve."

"It's okay," I say. "Nothing happened."

"It almost did," he says softly, his voice rough.

Be sensible, Faye. Try to be sensible.

"An attraction between us isn't so surprising. We're both young and decent-looking. We share similar passions and interests. We're both ambitious." I give him a polite smile. "The key, I guess, is not to give in to it. Mixing business and pleasure is never a good idea. I'm sure you agree with me."

"I do."

"So that's that," I say. "But, you know, we could still be friends."

"That would be great," he says, then purses his lips. "Except, I generally don't want to kiss my friends."

A flash of something almost unbearably wonderful courses through me and it takes an enormous amount of strength to remain impassive.

"If we ignore it," I suggest pragmatically, "I'm sure it'll go away."

"Has that worked for you in the past?" he asks me, taking bottles of North Star vodka and North Star vanilla vodka out from under the bar and placing them between us.

"I've…" I stare at the bottles, admiring the cream-colored silk scarf on the label of the vanilla bottle and wondering why no one else has done that yet. My eyes slide from the bottle, up his chest, to his face, and I answer him honestly: "I've never been in a situation like this before."

"This is a male-dominated business. You must meet men all the time, all over the world."

"I do. I'm just not…" *attracted to them.*

He stares at me intently before asking, "Why is this different?"

"Honestly? I don't know for sure." He pours a bit of the vodka in the shot glass, and I toss it back expertly, savoring the burn on my tongue and throat. "Delicious."

"Thank you. Please answer my question," he insists.

Fine. You want to talk to someone, Faye? Talk to him.

I place my elbows on the bar and lean forward.

"You make my favorite vodka, and I met you by chance, in a Chinese restaurant, on Christmas Eve. You came back to apologize for being such a jerk, and I almost threw up on your boots. We realized over Christmas dinner that we were already on one another's radars, and we're both struggling to connect, or reconnect, with siblings we've lost along the way." I gulp softly, searching his eyes. "Choose one reason, Trevor. Choose them all. We connected. It just…happened. This situation—you and me—isn't typical or ordinary. It's been…exceptional. Right from the start."

"And your answer to something this exceptional is for us to be…*friends?*" His tone is just short of angry, and I start to wonder if addressing our attraction head-on was wise.

That said, I try to stay the course: Sensible. Pragmatic.

"My answer to labeling a relationship between two people who met by chance, enjoy one another's company, may enter into a business agreement, but have no possible future together?" I nod. "Yes. I think friends is generous. I think anything else would be foolish."

He inhales sharply. "*No possible future?*"

I blink at him. "What?"

"You said that we have no possible future together."

"I don't see one...do you?"

"I don't like being sidelined before I start problem-solving." He purses his lips, and I think he might be pouting. "Being asked to be your friend sounds like forced castration." I gasp softly, and he shrugs. "I'm just being honest."

I blink at him. "As you pointed out, the timing is—"

"Something we can deal with."

"And working together?"

"Isn't guaranteed."

"So what are you saying?" I ask him.

"I don't know," he says, picking up the vanilla vodka with one hand and running the other through his thick, dark hair.

Alcohol. I need some.

"Trevor, I'm incredibly out of my depth. Pour the vanilla, please."

He does. He fills the shot glass in front of me, then reaches under the bar for another and fills his own.

"Do you want a ride to the Chalet Blanche when we're done here?" he asks, flattening his hands on the bar, his mint-green eyes boring into mine.

"Yes," I say. "Thank you."

"Will you come to my place for dinner tomorrow night?"

Yes!

"It's not a good idea," I tell him.

"I don't care," he says, raising his glass. "Will you come?"

Our situation, which I was trying to diffuse, has only grown more volatile in the last ten minutes, and I feel that spinning and falling sensation inside of me again, though I'm not certain of what it means or what its outcome will be.

I don't know what's happening between us because it's never happened to me before.

I don't know if we'll end up as friends or business associates or—*God help me*—in bed together.

I only know two things for sure:

> 1. I *cannot* say no to Trevor Starling, and
> 2. I *must* cancel my date with Mr. Fairbanks on Friday.

I lift my glass and clink it softly against his. "Yes. I would love to come to dinner tomorrow night."

CHAPTER EIGHT

Trevor

The drive from the Chalet Blanche back to my house is almost half an hour, so I have plenty of time to think after I drop her off.

I don't want to have or develop feelings for Faye Findley.

Tough shit, my heart whispers. *Too late.*

I don't know how she's gotten so far under my skin in three days, but she has. *So far*, in fact, that I have to seriously reconsider what I'm about to do with Faith Crawford this weekend. I stopped myself from kissing Faye in the distillery because I still feel a sense of obligation to Faith that predates my acquaintance with Faye, but when I said that "bad timing" is something that can be dealt with, I was thinking about canceling on Faith.

God knows how much I want to have sex. And Faith is a prearranged, drama-free, no-strings-attached, guaranteed fling. It couldn't be easier. It's a sure-fucking-thing. But— *fuck me five ways from Sunday*—I don't think I *want* to sleep with Faith.

In a twist of fate I never, ever could have imagined, I think I'd rather hold out for Faye Findley.

The language of my ad couldn't have been clearer: *Zero*

chance of love. So what's Faye Findley, then? She's the less-than-zero chance. Because she's making me feel things that I haven't felt since those early, precious days with Marlena.

She's making me *feel* again.

So what exactly is my responsibility to Faith Crawford?

A live, in-person apology, for sure, and remuneration.

I don't know where she's coming from, but presumably, she's purchased an airline ticket to make the trip. She may or may not have taken time off from work, but I probably should assume she has. I prepaid the five-hundred-dollars-a-night suite at the Chalet Blanche, and I'll transfer the reservation to her name so that she can stay if she wants to. Additionally, I'll prepay a thousand dollars at the spa so that she can schedule whatever services she'd like. All in? I probably owe her five thousand dollars in travel and lost wages, in addition to whatever I'll end up paying the Chalet Blanche. About eight thousand dollars.

It's a large amount of money, but not beyond my means.

And something tells me that it'll be the easiest check I ever wrote.

That said, showing up at the Chalet Blanche on Friday night to cancel our plans in person is going to suck. But once I do? I'm free. I'll be free to do whatever I like with Faye Findley.

Not that she's left anything on the table. I grunt in frustration, recalling both her offer to be friends and her assertion that we have no possible future.

And both *piss…me…off.*

But Faye Findley doesn't know yet that I'm a man who appreciates a challenge. That, and I'm just as driven as she is. When I see something I want, I figure out how to make it mine. And what I want…is her.

***

I shower, shave, and dress in jeans, a white T-shirt, and a black cashmere V-neck sweater, hurrying myself along so that I'm in my car by four thirty to pick up Faye. I check myself out in the bathroom mirror, considering my appearance and deciding I look okay.

My goal for tonight is to spend time with Faye Findley without actually making a move on her. And I don't kid myself that it'll be easy. I'm not sure I've ever been as attracted to anyone like I am to Faye. I'm longing to take her hair out of that tight, thick bun and run my hands through it. I'm dying to watch her dark eyes widen with pleasure. I want to see it. I want to make it happen.

Adjusting myself behind the zipper of my jeans, I remind myself for the hundredth time that nothing should happen tonight. Not until after I've spoken to Faith Crawford tomorrow evening.

But that doesn't mean I've skimped on preparations.

On my way to the garage, I stop in the kitchen to check on dinner.

This afternoon, while Baz manned the office and tasting room, I made reindeer meatballs with a Swedish cream sauce. They've been simmering in my Crock-Pot for hours and make my house smell awesome. I'll complement them with some homemade highbush-cranberry jam—the

Alaskan answer to lingonberries—made by my mother. I have red-eye potatoes cut up and seasoned, waiting to be put on a cookie sheet and broiled, and for dessert, I stopped by the Fudge Pot and picked up an assortment of local fudges. My favorite is bright purple, colored that way because it's made with Alaskan blueberries, and hand to God, it's the most delicious thing I've ever eaten. Especially when paired with blueberry vodka, something I've been working on for the last few weeks and want to share with Faye tonight.

Rubbing my hands together with anticipation, I head downstairs, jump in my car, and pull out of the garage to make the drive to the Chalet Blanche. En route, my phone rings, and without looking at the console, I press answer.

"Hello?"

"Trev! Don't hang up."

I'd know my brother's voice anywhere. Even after six months of not speaking.

I clench my jaw and crack the window, breathing deeply.

"What do you want, Cez?"

"We, um...we missed you at Christmas." He clears his throat. "Mom says you stopped by the farm yesterday."

I don't say anything. I'm not going to make this easier for Cez by encouraging him.

"Um...and she said that when she mentioned Marlena, you didn't...I mean, you didn't leave or get pissed or..."

It's starting to snow, so I turn on my wipers. I'm still waiting for him to say something that needs or deserves an answer.

"Trev? You still there?"

"Mm-hm. But I'm going to lose you in a second."

"Heading out of town?"

I sigh loudly. He doesn't need to know my plans. "Is there something you needed, Cecil?"

"I just...I hate how things are. I miss you. I didn't mean to hurt you. I want...I want you to know I'm sorry. Marlena's sorry. We didn't mean to..."

"What? Fuck each other? Fuck me over?"

"Trev," he whispers. "Please."

"Please what?"

"Please forgive me."

My eyes water. I hate it that they do, but I can't help it. They burn, and I blink them furiously, opening the window a little more.

"I have to go."

"Please, Trev," he whimpers, and suddenly, I remember him as a little kid—maybe three or four—falling out a of a tree and breaking his arm. *Get Mama. Please, Trev. I hurting.*

He's hurting again now. I can hear it. I can feel it.

But *I'm* hurting too. And he was the one who broke my heart.

"I'm...not ready to talk yet," I say, the words rough and raspy because I'm swallowing back tears.

My little brother clears his throat, likely doing the same. "Yeah. Yeah, okay. I, um, I understand."

"Another time," I say. "Maybe."

"Another time would be good," he says, hope infusing his voice as he sniffles once, then sighs.

"Bye, Cez."

"Take care, Trev."

I hit the End button on the console, staring at the road in front of me.

It's the first time since that terrible night in Portland that we've spoken. Not that he hasn't tried to contact me since, but I haven't picked up or answered his texts.

It hurt to hear his voice. It hurt to hear him say he wants forgiveness, but it still makes me angry to hear him apologize. *I didn't mean to hurt you. I want you to know I'm sorry.* These words ring phony to me. I'm not ready to believe them. Not yet.

And yet…

I miss Cez.

While Baz is thoughtful, sensitive, and introspective, Cez is easygoing, carefree, and fun. I remember Faye's question from yesterday about Cez and Marlena getting together being a "best-case scenario" for me, and suddenly, a memory surfaces from last Christmas.

My mom put on the Will Ferrell movie *Elf*, and I rolled my eyes as the theme song started, relocating from the TV room to the kitchen with my laptop. While I built a spreadsheet comparing the first two years of holiday sales, Cez and Marlena sat side by side on the couch, drinking beer, throwing popcorn at each other, and laughing their asses off at Buddy's fish-out-of-water elf antics.

At the time, I'd noticed their carrying-on with affection, chalking it up to future in-laws bonding, but maybe it was just…joy.

Maybe they were falling in love with each other right there on the couch, watching a dumb holiday movie together. Certainly they were connecting. Anyone could see that. But as I think back on it now, I realize it was…*more*. It was that heady, all-consuming *joy* of someone "getting" you, loving what you love, laughing at what you think is funny, and being present to enjoy it.

I wasn't present.

I didn't love what she loved.

I didn't laugh at what she thought was funny.

Marlena wasn't serious enough for me, and I wasn't enough fun for her.

But Cez? With his easygoing temperament and teasing blue eyes? He was perfect her—*is* perfect for her.

Maybe I can't blame them for falling in love. Maybe they were *meant* for each other, and my role, in the grand scheme of things, was to be the bridge that brought them together.

Oh, but how I wish they'd figured out a way to tell me instead of cheating, instead of making me look like an idiot, instead of blindsiding me on the day before my wedding. Couldn't they have sat me down and explained? Couldn't they have tried?

But when I think of them, two young-at-heart, fun-loving, nonconfrontational personalities faced with telling me an unfortunate truth? Maybe they just couldn't figure out how to speak up, how to tell me. Maybe they wanted to— even meant to—a million times but couldn't find the right time, the right way, the right words to shatter my heart. I know I loom large as Cez's older brother, and with a significant age different between me and Marlena, I was the dominant partner in our relationship too.

Is it possible that I was so unapproachable to them that they couldn't figure out a way to tell me? Maybe. When I really think about the dynamics at play between us, it doesn't seem impossible. And it may even be my path to forgiveness.

When I pull up at the Chalet Blanche, I find that a conversation with the potential to ruin my night…hasn't. In fact, I think I am more at peace with Cez and Marlena than I've been in months, and it makes me breathe easier and feel more whole again.

I look up in time to see Faye Findley step out of the inn wearing high boots and her fur-trimmed parka.

Framed by the soft white light over the French doors, I'm positive I've never seen another woman more beautiful. All thoughts of Cez and Marlena and *Elf* and last Christmas fly swiftly away.

All I can see…all I *want* to see…is her.

***

Faye

The expression on his Trevor's face as he rounds the car and opens my door is…intoxicating.

In the simplest possible terms:

He is hunting. I'm his prey.

And I hope to God he catches me.

His eyes are dark, with just a thin circle of green around onyx pupils, and he smells heavenly—like something homecooked and delicious mixed with freshly showered man.

"Hey," he says.

I lean up on tiptoes and kiss each of his cheeks in turn.

"Hi. Thanks for picking me up."

When my feet are flat on the ground again, he stares into my eyes with an intensity that might intimidate other women but doesn't faze me. We bonded over spirits, T and I, which made the playing field level from the very beginning.

"My pleasure."

He opens my door, and I step into the car, settling in comfortably as he shuts my door and tips the doorman for waiting with me.

I've had all day to think about him, and this is what I've decided: I like him. I like him more than I've liked another man, well, ever. And I'm not going to squander this chance to get to know him better. I think about Harry telling me that Austin was going to kiss her, and I feel certain that— sooner or later—Trevor will do the same. And I've already decided: I will let him, and I will kiss him back.

Last night, as I lay in bed staring up at the ceiling, I went over and over our conversation at the tasting room bar, specifically two parts to which he took exception: being friends and having no future. And when I forced myself to be honest, I had to confess that he's not alone. I don't want to be friends either—I want far more than that. And though I have no gift for predicting the future, I hate the idea of shutting one down before we even have a chance to explore it.

I remember my initial feeling about Mr. Fairbanks' assertion that there would be "zero chance of love" between himself and his applicant of choice—I felt sorry for him. At the time, I reminded myself that while finding love had proved a challenge for me as well, unlike him, I wasn't ready to give up on it yet.

So why would I predict "no future" for us? Why would I give up on the possibility of something happening with Trevor Starling, the first man for whom I've ever had feelings this *strong*, this…*good?*

Well, I won't. I regret what I said yesterday, and I won't be renewing those sentiments any time soon.

In a turn of events I never, ever saw coming, I even conceded to myself that I'd be willing to lose North Star as a potential acquisition if it meant that our personal relationship had some time and space to develop. And yes, that realization felt awfully strange, because I've never prioritized my personal life over my business life—not when my parents passed away and not for my little sister, who has needed me over the years—but I think it's my recent revelations about my relationship with Harry that have opened my mind.

I want to give Trevor Starling a chance.

I don't know what that will look like or where it will go. Hell, we could discover tonight that we can't stand each other and go our separate ways. But whatever happens, I don't want to regret shutting something down before allowing it to evolve.

He sits down beside me, glancing at me before turning

over the engine.

"I like your boots."

I grin. "Thanks."

"And your hair."

Instead of pulling it back tightly, I blow-dried it upside down to give it some volume and wave, then twisted it into a looser, more romantic bun than usual. A few tendrils even got free and I left them to frame my face, which I made up with a little mascara, eyeliner, and lipstick. Under my coat, I'm wearing a simple gray sweater dress with pearls. I'm no femme fatale, but I know how to put a little extra effort into my appearance. After all, I've been on the list for every major Boston gala for years.

"Thank you."

"You look...*beautiful*, Faye."

"Do I detect a note of surprise?" I ask as I buckle my seat belt.

"Not surprised," he says. "Just...appreciative."

"Well, I could hardly come to your house for dinner in sweats."

"You could've," he says, pulling away from the hotel. "I wouldn't have minded."

"You deserve better than that," I tell him. "It was nice of you to invite me over."

"I hope you like Swedish meatballs," he says, grinning at me.

"I love them," I say. "I adore Scandinavia in general."

"I haven't been."

"Put it on your list," I suggest. "Right under New

York."

"Will do," he says, offering me a full-bodied smile, full of promise, as he puts the car in gear and we leave the Chalet Blanche behind.

***

Three hours later, I've taken a leisurely tour of Trevor's stunning house, eaten the most delicious meatballs I've ever tasted and enjoyed three glasses of a truly exquisite Montepulciano.

"What time do the northern lights start?" I ask him.

He chuckles. "It's not like a concert or TV show. You can't predict solar activity. But! The snow stopped, which is good. The sky's clear. If we turn off all the lights and take a seat on the couch…" He gestures to a sofa set back a few feet from floor-to-ceiling picture windows that flank a massive fireplace. "We may be able to catch them sometime after ten o'clock."

"Sounds good," I tell him. "What do we do until then?"

His eyes flick to my lips, as they have many times tonight, before they skim back up to my eyes. "Ready for dessert?"

"Sure."

I get the feeling he's using even more self-control than he did yesterday, and I still wish I knew the reason. *Why* is the timing bad? And when he said it could be overcome, did he mean *immediately*? Or eventually? Because I'm *all* for the immediate option, especially since I'm expected back in Boston on the second.

"I had an idea," he says, hopping up to take our dirty

plates to the kitchen and returning with a lavender silk tie in his hands.

I eye it, then slide my uncertain gaze to him. "*What*…exactly?"

"How do you feel about being blindfolded?"

"Should I have decided feelings about it?"

He chuckles. "Are you up for it?"

"Yes…" I say slowly, "though I'd like to know why."

"I've been playing with different vodka infusions," he explains, gently tying the Trevor-scented silk around my head, before leaning forward to whisper in my ear, "and I'd like your opinion."

I swear his lips brush the shell of my ear, and a shiver darts down my spine, stealing my breath away. "I, uh…sure. I can…give it. M-my opinion."

"Faye." His voice is a low rumble, and I imagine I can feel his breath kiss my cheek.

With everything dark, my other senses are heightened. "Yes?"

"I didn't know how hot this would be."

"Having me blindfolded?"

"Having you blindfolded."

Muscles deep inside of my body—muscles that I am only aware of when I am touching myself under the covers—flex and contract, and I gasp softly.

I know he hears me because he laughs before stepping away, his footsteps retreating back into the kitchen. There's the sound of the refrigerator opening—no, the freezer, I think—and then closing again. A plate or platter is placed on the marble counter. A moment later, he's coming closer to me. A chair scrapes the hardwood floor.

"Faye, I'm going to move your chair a little, okay?"

He's right. This is hot. "Mm-hm."

As I sit tight, my chair is tilted back, angled a different way, and then tilted forward again. A moment later, his knees touch mine.

"I'm sitting across from you," he says.

"I know."

"Are you ready?"

"I'm…breathless." I don't know what to do with my hands. I fold them, then flatten them on my lap, my nails curling into the exposed skin between the hem of my dress and the tops of my boots.

"I can see," he says, his voice soft and low as his hands reach out for mine. He clutches them gently, and I savor the rough warmth of them. "Just breathe."

I would've guessed that Trevor touching me would make me more nervous, but it doesn't. My fingers move gingerly to thread themselves through his, and I breathe in and out, deep, soothing breaths that calm me.

"You need your hands and I need mine." His fingers retract, leaving mine alone, for which I am momentarily sorry. "Ready?"

"Mmm," I hum. "Yes."

"Okay. I'm going to give you a shot glass with an infused vodka. Take a sip. Then I'll offer you a piece of fudge. Taste them together. And you can decide when to sip again, okay?"

How delightful. "Yes."

The glass he places in my hands, which has been chilled in the freezer, is icy cold, with a sheen of frost on the sides. I take a sip, letting the cold alcohol swirl in my mouth as his hand nudges mine with a small piece of fudge. I wait a moment to eat it, identifying the vodka as infused with a kind of berry. It's subtle, just a little sweet and utterly divine.

"Oh, my God. Yes. What is this?"

He chuckles softly. "Eat the fudge."

I pop the sweet in my mouth, and I swear, it's a taste explosion like I've never tried before.

"Ahhhh. Ohhhh," I sigh. "Oh, my God. Mmmm."

"Jesus, Faye," he half-grunts, half-whispers.

"It's *so* good," I murmur, taking another sip of the berry vodka. "Oh, my God, that's…that's delicious."

He adjusts himself on the seat across from me. I can tell by the way his knees lose contact with mine for a second.

"You, um, liked it," he finally says.

"Mm-hmmmm. I can still taste it. Amazing."

I'm expecting him to tell me that another tasting pair is coming, but instead, I feel his finger touch down lightly on my head, and a moment later, the blindfold is gone. I blink my eyes against the light, looking around the room to find Trevor already in the kitchen standing behind the counter.

"What happened?" I ask, glancing at the table where two more shot glasses and two more pieces of fudge are waiting. "No more?"

He clears his throat, flattening his hands on the counter between us and staring down at them.

"What?" I ask, standing up from my chair and stepping around the counter to stand across from him. "Is something wrong?"

"No." He looks up. "I'm just…hiding."

"From me?"

"I didn't expect for your reaction to…" He bites his lower lip, then winces. "It turned me on. A lot. In an obvious way."

Is he talking about getting an erection? Holy crap, I think he is.

"It did?"

"Do you hear yourself when you drink something you like? It's…*orgasmic*, Faye. I mean, game over. It's crazy sexy."

A flush starts in my breasts, trailing up my chest to my neck and finally to my cheeks, trailing down over the flat plane of my belly to my core, to my sex. I'm hot. I'm wet. I'm turned on too.

"Oh fuck," he mutters. "And now you look like it too."

"Look like what?"

"Like we just had sex." He leans forward to tuck a tendril of hair behind my ear and grins at my expression. "But your eyes are so wide. How do you do that?"

"Do what?"

"Look so innocent. When you were *made* to be…" His voice trails off and he swallows.

"To be?" My voice is so soft, it's just shy of a squeak.

"Fucked," he whispers.

My breath catches, but instead of recoiling, as I might if I felt insulted, I lean forward just a touch. I can't look away from him. I don't want to.

"Probably because I've never been," I hear myself saying.

Faye! Faye, what the hell are you doing?

But it's too late. The words are already out there…as evidenced by his reaction: his mouth drops open his brows knit together, and his eyes narrow. He stares at me. Hard. "Excuse me?"

I have no idea what to say. My mind is a blank. I stare back at him and say nothing.

"You've never been…" he murmurs.

I lick my lips, gathering my senses together, and leaning away from him as my cheeks redden from a different emotion all together.

"Faye, you've never been…"

"Fucked."

He blinks at me. "Are you saying you're a…*virgin?*"

I've been here before. Not many times, but once or twice, and it has never gone well from here. In my previous experience, men are either turned off or intimidated by this information, and their first response is almost always to verify my age, then ask how it's possible that I'm *still* a virgin. It's an exercise in humiliation that yes, I have brought on myself tonight, but that no, I cannot bear.

"You said you hadn't had a relationship in a while, but I never thought…"

I take a deep breath and muster a polite smile. "Tonight has been just lovely. Thank you for having me to your home. I can call an Uber if you've had too much to drink—"

"Where are you going?"

"Back to my hotel."

"Why?"

"Because your next question is to ask me my age, followed by an inquisition about how I am still a virgin at thirty years old, and frankly, I can't stomach it. I enjoyed myself so much tonight and I'd just prefer to—"

"Faye," he says.

"What?"

"Shut up," he tells me, rounding the counter, drawing me into his arms and dropping his lips to mine.

I arch my back and lean my head back, giving him better access to my mouth, which he covers with his, his lips moving softly but insistently over mine. With a soft whimper, I open mine, meeting his tongue as it slips between my lips. His arms tighten around me and my hands, which are flattened against his chest, slide up to his jaw. I hold his face in my hands as he kisses me, as he explores my mouth with the velvet heat of his tongue.

He makes a sound—half groan, half growl—as he backs me up against the kitchen counter, still ravishing my mouth with his. My arms loop around his neck. My nipples harden into stiff points under my sweater dress. And heats pools in my belly, telling me how much I want him, that my body—heretofore unknown to a man—is ready for an introduction.

When he leans away from me, I wait a second before slowly opening my eyes. His are wide and dark, staring fiercely down at mine, as the evidence of his aforementioned arousal prods my stomach in a way that only makes me want to keep going.

I press my body against his.

He grins at me. "No more for now."

"Why not?"

"I need a day."

"Just a day?" I ask.

"Just a day," he promises, brushing his lips against my forehead. "But I want to pick you up on Friday morning. I want you to check out of your hotel and spend New Year's weekend here with me."

"I want that too," I whisper, resting my cheek against his chest.

"So that's a yes?" he confirms.

"Mm-hm. Definitely a yes." I breathe in his scent before leaning back to look into his eyes. "I didn't expect that. A kiss." *Such a good kiss.*

"I didn't want you to go yet," he says.

"I won't. I'll stay a while longer," I promise, leaning back to look up at him.

"Didn't you want to see the northern lights?" he asks, still holding me tightly, his lips tilted up in a whisper of a sexy smile. "I've still got some vodka and fudge for you to try."

"I'd like that," I say, smiling up at him, my heart still racing from the best kiss I've ever had.

He lets me go but takes my hand, leading me to the couch by the windows. "Then follow me, Faye Findley."

And I think to myself,

Anywhere.

CHAPTER NINE

Faye

When I wake up the next morning, it's still dark, but I'm very warm and cozy, and for a moment, I think I'm back at the North Pole Inn, except I'm not.

My subconscious insists that I'm not.

My eyes flutter open slowly, and I realize that I'm not alone—there's an arm thrown over my hip and a strong, steady chest pushes rhythmically into my back with deep, sleepy breaths.

Trevor.

Sigh.

We must have fallen asleep watching the northern lights last night and have somehow ended up—*both still fully dressed, of course!*—spooned together on his couch.

And. It's. Heaven.

I should probably wake him up and make him drive me back to my hotel, but instead, I snuggle closer to him, savoring the warmth of his body pressed intimately up against mine. The dead weight of his arm over my hip and his hand flattened on my stomach feels possessive in a way that thrills me. I've never slept a night with a man like this, but I could certainly get used to it: surrounded by his scent and warm body? Yes, I could get used to it very quickly, given the chance.

But then I think about what today holds, and my heart sinks a little.

I tried to write an email to Mr. Fairbanks yesterday—to let him know that I needed to back out of our agreement. But around three o'clock, I got a message from him, confirming that he'd meet me in the lobby of the Chalet Blanche this evening, holding a red rose. And suddenly, I knew how cowardly it would be to cancel our plans via email and not show up to speak to him in person.

That said? I dread it.

I've had to fire many people over my ten years as the head of Findley Imports, but it's never gotten easier or more palatable to me. I don't like delivering bad news. But who does? Letting someone look you in the eye as you hurt them, I've learned, is an important nonverbal way to take responsibility for your decisions and actions.

Mr. Fairbanks didn't do anything wrong—he deserves an explanation *from* me, and he has the right to share his anger and disappointment *with* me.

Thank God I have New Year's weekend with Trevor to look forward to. Thinking of those three days with him will give me the strength and composure I'll need to let Mr. Fairbanks know that I am entirely in the wrong and very sorry that I'm no longer able to meet the terms of our agreement.

In regard to my financial responsibility to him, I've decided to offer to reimburse him the cost of the suite at the

Chalet Blanche—about $1,500 for three nights—plus the cost of the ad he placed and any medical tests he paid for out-of-pocket. It's the least I can do for ruining his New Year's celebration.

It feels like cold comfort, to offer him a check for $2,000, but the feelings I have for T, new though they are, make it impossible for me to be intimate with Mr. Fairbanks...or any other man, for that matter. I *only* want to be with Trevor. I know we just met. And I don't know what will end up happening between us. I only know that for now—*right now*—he's what I want.

"Are you awake?"

His sleepy voice rumbles close to my ear and makes me smile.

I turn in his arms to look at him, our noses almost touching, the fronts of our body flush against each other.

"Yes."

"You think very loudly," he says, leaning forward to press his lips to my nose.

"That's impossible," I inform him. "Thoughts have no sound."

"Yours do." He glances at my lips and sighs before sliding his eyes up to mine. "I like you a lot, Faye Findley."

My heart. Oh, my heart. I don't know that it's ever been quite this full.

"I like you a lot too."

He grins at me, tightening the arm that's still around me. "Do I recall correctly that you promised to spend New Year's with me? Here? In my home?"

"You do."

"For said weekend together, would you like to avail yourself of my guest room or...?"

I stare at him for a second, a tiny smile dying to turn up the corners of my mouth. "Or?"

"Share my bed with me?"

My stomach explodes with butterflies.

"Option two," I say, "please."

This time, he misses my nose when he leans forward to kiss me and presses his lips to my mouth instead. It's quick and it's sweet, and it leaves me wanting so much more.

"That's my preference too," he says. "Though...can we very quickly touch on something you mentioned last night?"

My stomach drops and my smile vanishes. My fucking virginity. Damn it. Why the hell did I blurt that out?

"Faye," he says, capturing my eyes with his. "It's a big deal."

"It's not. There are many things I've never done with my body. I've never bungee jumped. I've never taken drugs. I've never stuck a Q-tip in my ear."

"Fair enough," he says. "And I get that it's personal and you don't want to discuss it, but I just wanted to say...I just wanted you to know...that nothing will happen unless you want it to, okay? If you want to sleep like this, fully clothed, I'm cool with that. If you want to be more...intimate, that's fine with me too. You're in charge, Faye. I'll follow your lead."

I'm so touched by this short speech, unexpected tears burn my eyes, and I blink them back, leaning forward to touch my forehead to his.

"Thank you," I say. "Whatever happens, thank you for that."

"How about some breakfast before I drive you back to your hotel?" he asks, sliding his arm from my hip and leaning up on his elbow.

"Sure," I say. "I'd love it."

***

Since I won't be seeing Trevor for the rest of today, I decide to make the most of my hotel while I'm there for one more day and night. I have an eleven o'clock deep-tissue massage, and a delectable lunch of seared salmon, rice pilaf, and sautéed root vegetables is delivered to my room at one, with Baked Alaska for desert (which, I'm slightly disappointed to discover, is really just a fancy name for ice cream cake with browned merengue on top).

After lunch, I have a two o'clock conference call with Karl, my head of acquisitions, with whom I discuss North Star Spirits.

"It's not that I'm backing off, Karl," I tell him. "I'm just saying we can live without another craft vodka company on our roster right now."

"You weren't impressed?"

"I was. I am. The Starlings have a great operation and a terrific product. But Mr. Starling isn't eager to sell, and I'm okay waiting until they need a partner for a cash infusion. At that point, we can offer to take them to the next level. But for now, at least, they seem content as is." I pause for a second, then add, "Let's leave it alone."

"Okay. Got it." I can hear papers rustling. "So this is interesting. Had a call from UNNW this morning."

"United Northwest?"

UNNW, United Northwest Distributors, would be a major rival of Findley Imports except we're located in Boston and they're in Seattle. They do for the West Coast what we do in the East. But we are both privately owned beverage importation and distribution companies with a three-generation history; in fact, my grandfather was acquaintances with Rodolfo Castillo, who started UNNW.

"Yeah."

"What did they want?"

"You know that old Mr. Castillo passed away several years ago, right? Well, his son, Santino, had a stroke last month and joined his father. It turns out the grandson, Florian, isn't interested in keeping the family business going. He wants to sell. Anyway, his mother remembered her husband working with your father and asked him to call you before anyone else."

"Are you saying that UNNW is for sale?"

Karl chuckles. "I'm saying that the perfect way for Findley Imports to have a West Coast presence just presented itself on a silver platter, yes."

I squeal in excitement, jumping off the bed I'm sitting on and doing a little jig in my hotel bathrobe. "Are you kidding?"

"Would I play with you like that?"

"My father always dreamed of us being bicoastal! This is big, Karl. This is huge!"

"So I take it you want to set up a meeting?"

"Whenever Florian Castillo is ready. I'm in Alaska for a few more days, so it's no problem for me to get down to Seattle. Quick flight back and forth. Contact Carlene. She's got my schedule."

"You got it, boss."

"And Karl, not a word to anyone. If we can manage a private sale, the acquisition and merger will be that much more seamless."

"Alrighty, Faye. Sounds good."

I hang up with Karl, brimming with excitement and…I have no one to share it with.

Although Trevor would certainly understand the fantastic implications of such a merger, I won't see him until tomorrow. Hmm. Harry doesn't take much of a role in the business of Findley Imports, but she *is* my sister, and I want to share this with someone.

I dial her number.

"Faye!"

"Harry! How's Vail?"

"It's great. The rest of the crew went skiing today, but I stayed behind to catch up on some school work. How's Alaska?"

"Much better than expected. What happened with Austin?"

"Well…I thought about it and realized you were right. He didn't really like me. I think I was just convenient. And I don't want to make out with someone because it's convenient for them. Not anymore. I want it to be…special.

So I've been friendly to Austin, but not, um, *available*…if you know what I mean."

"I know exactly what you mean, and I think you made the right decision." I pause for a second, remembering my conversation with Trevor this morning. "Harry…your first time. Was it…special?"

"Faye!"

"I know we haven't talked about things like that in the past, but I want you to know that I'm here for you. For anything."

She sighs. "No. It wasn't special."

This news hurts my heart in a way I wouldn't have expected, and I wince, standing up and walking to the window, where I have a beautiful view of the white mountains in the distance.

"How did it happen?"

"I was at a party. Drunk. He was in my AP English class, and I thought he was sweet."

High school. She's talking about her junior year. She lost her virginity almost four years ago, and I had no idea.

"He wasn't?"

"He wasn't anything. We barely knew each other. It was sloppy and messy and over almost the moment it started."

"But you gave consent!" I bark, worry making my heart beat faster. "Didn't you?"

"I didn't say no. I didn't push him away. I just thought it would be different than it was." She's quiet for a second. "Stupid."

"Not stupid." Just…alone. I ache for Harry, who didn't

have a mother *or* a big sister to guide and comfort her. "I'm so sorry I wasn't there for you, Harry."

"It's okay," she says. She laughs lightly. "It's gotten a lot better since."

"You've had many partners?"

"I wouldn't say many. No more than most other girls my age." She clears her throat. "Though I don't think I'll be adding Austin to that list. I liked your advice. I might move a little slower in the future, you know? I mean, I'm not looking for my forever someone right now, but a boyfriend might be nice, and I don't think I'm going to find him if I make out with anyone who shows interest."

"Whatever you decide to do," I tell her, "I'm here for you. I promise, Harry. And I'm so sorry I haven't been as available before now."

"You've been busy," she points out, "looking after Findley Imports." She clears her throat. "You know, I've always thought of you as the guardian of *two* siblings: one older, with lots of special needs, and then…me."

Again, that crushing feeling clenches my heart, because she never should have felt less important than our family's business.

"Oh, Harry. I'm so—"

"No!" she exclaims. "No, don't apologize. I'm not trying to make you feel bad! I admire you, Faye. I remember Daddy's devotion to the company—the way Mama would keep his dinner warm for hours and hours while he finished a long workday at the office. He worked long hours, and I had Mama at home. When they died, you were left alone with e-everything. The c-company…m-me…" Her voice catches. "I'm not m-mad at you, Faye."

But she's crying. I can hear it, and it makes my eyes burn too. I'm mad at me. I'm *furious* with me. I was left with her and the business, but I was an adult. She had only me. And she didn't *even* have me. I was too busy for her.

"Oh, Harry."

"I mean it, Faye! I'm not mad at you. I hope I can be half the businesswoman you are someday."

"I just hope you can be a better human being," I whisper.

"Don't do that," she chastises me. "Don't devalue what you've been able to do. And Faye…you weren't unkind to me. You weren't mean. You made sure that I was safe and cared for. You were just busy."

She's right. I was just busy. But still…I could've done better. "I *will* do better."

"You already are," she says softly, sniffling. "I love you, Faye."

"I love you too, Harry," I tell her for the first time in years. And it feels good—so very, very good—to feel this closeness, this intimacy, this *love* between me and my only sibling. "I love you so much."

She giggles through tears. "Me too!"

I join her, laughing through our tears and celebrating the fact that it's never too late for family to forgive each other, to make the most of the time they have left with each other, whether it's a little or a lot. And I hope—I fervently hope—that Harry and I have a lot of time left to love each

166

other.

"I have to go," she says. "This paper is due the week I get back."

"Want to meet me in Boston next week?" I ask her. "Before you go back to school?"

"Definitely," she says. "I need to see this new Faye in person."

"New Faye?"

"Mm-hm," she hums. "Everything about my big sister feels new this Christmas. It's the best gift I've ever received."

"Well, I'll have Carlene book you a ticket to see New Faye before you go back to school," I tell her. "Work hard. I'll see you soon, little sister."

"Bye, Faye. Talk soon!"

When we hang up, I realize that I didn't tell her about the possible merger with UNNW, which was the entire reason for my call. I also realize that I'm one hundred percent okay with that.

I love you, Faye.

I love you too, Harry.

Business can wait.

***

At six o'clock, I take a deep breath, get in the shower, and start preparing for my unfortunate meeting with Mr. Fairbanks in the lobby of the hotel at seven o'clock.

With the picture I sent to him propped up on the bathroom counter, I blow-dry my hair upside down, freeing the natural wave and curl so that it looks like it did in the photo. He won't really have seen my face, since I'm wearing oversized Chanel sunglasses in the picture, but I make it up with eyeliner, mascara, dark eyeshadow, and a redder-than-usual lipstick that I think Harry would choose. Because I was wearing a white bikini top and denim shorts in the photo, I pull on jeans and a white blouse, which I leave open to reveal a touch of cleavage.

When I check out my reflection in the mirror, I look nothing like myself—like Faye Findley with her hair pulled back in a bun and her drab, sensible clothes. I've done a pretty fair job of recreating the fun-loving, breezy girl from the picture, and as a result, I look a few years younger and a lot more carefree than I actually am.

Checking the time on my phone, my heart bumps into a faster rhythm when I find an email message from Mr. Fairbanks saying he's downstairs waiting for me whenever I'm ready to meet him.

"Get it over with," I tell my reflection, checking myself out one more time and deciding I look as close to the picture as I'm likely to get. I shove my keycard in my hip pocket, put my white sunglasses on top of my head as a hairband, and slip out the door of my room.

***

Trevor

I'm standing in the chic lobby of the Chalet Blanche, a long-stemmed red rose in one sweaty hand and the other shoved into the pocket of black tailored business pants.

I couldn't be more uncomfortable if I tried.

Every few seconds I glance around nervously, hoping that Faye Findley won't suddenly appear, wondering why the hell I'm here. Because if that happens? I honestly don't know what I'll do.

First, I'd feel embarrassed for her to know that I placed the ad in the first place. Aside from acting as my own personal pimp, the very act of soliciting consensual, no-strings-attached sex with a stranger feels cheap and sordid now, though it seemed like a perfectly harmless idea a month ago when I placed the ad.

Second, I wouldn't want Faye to think, even for a second, that I was cheating on her. I know. I know. Faye Findley and I are only in the very, very beginning of a relationship with one another and haven't outlined what that means yet. But minimally, it means that I'm not fucking some anonymous woman I met through a personal ad while courting her.

The net-net of these feelings is that I'm uneasy standing here, and every snap and crackle of the fire in the übermodern fireplace just about makes me jump. I'll be relieved once I've explained to Faith that I can't honor our agreement. And once I'm in my car, on the way back to my house? I'll be in a position to really explore the chemistry between me and a certain East Coast businesswoman who's promised to be all mine for New Year's.

Click-clack. Click-clack.

The sound of heeled shoes on the black marble floor alerts me to the fact that someone is approaching me from behind, and I turn slowly to find the woman from the photograph walking toward me.

Because she's glancing down as she makes her way to

me, I have a second to check her out, and as promised, she's stunning.

About five feet six inches tall in black, slingback heels, wearing tight, tapered jeans and a white blouse, she is as chic and classy in person as she was in her picture. Gold bracelets on her wrist and a gold-chain belt slung low on her hips catch the firelight as she approaches and give her a goddess-like aura. Her hair is loose and wild and, no doubt as an homage to her photo, she has a pair of white sunglasses perched on top of her head.

I hold my breath, still turning around slowly to greet her, eager to see her face because I know it's going to match the rest of her. I know she's going to be beautiful and rich, the sort of woman any man alive would want to——

She looks up.

W-w-wait.

My mouth drops.

Holy shit.

Her footsteps slow down.

No. No, no, no.

Her neck tilts to the side as she focuses on my face.

Fuck. No.

I blink at her, because…because…

"Faye?"

She stops about two feet away from me, frozen in her tracks, her eyes locked on mine and her lips parted in surprise. Her eyes widen, her eyebrows furrowing in confusion, then straightening out as understanding dawns.

"Trevor?" she whispers, her eyes darting to the flower

in my hand. "Are you…Mr. Fairbanks?"

My eyes narrow. The rose drops from my fingers, landing on the marble with a soft thud.

"*You're* Faith Crawford?" I practically spit.

Betrayal is a potent feeling in my current wheelhouse, and my brain is trying to decide if it applies here.

"C-Crawford is my…" The stricken look on her face mirrors the turmoil within me. "W-was my mother's maiden name. It's my middle name."

"And Faith?"

"Derivative of Faye."

I nod once, feeling foolish that I hadn't put the two names together before now, but damn it, *not once* did I think Faye was Faith or vice versa. I never suspected. Never even wondered. This whole time, they have subsisted in separate universes. Except now—*right now*—those universes are horrifically, preposterously colliding.

"What are you doing here? *Why* are you here?" I demand, knowing the answer to these questions but desperately seeking more information.

"Why are *you*?" she fires back.

"I'm here to meet Faith Crawford."

"Well, I'm here to meet Mr. Fairbanks."

"But *why*?" I yell. "*Why* would you answer the ad of—of some random man looking for sex?"

"Why do you *think*? Because I was looking for sex, obviously."

"You would *do* that? You would…you would give your *virginity* to some—some stranger that you didn't even—"

"Shut up!" she hisses as the front desk attendant clears her throat in our direction.

"Don't you have any self-respect?"

She gasps, the surprise on her face quickly segueing to anger. "Are you *kidding* me?"

"No," I say, straight-faced and utterly confused. "I'm not. I'm not fucking kidding."

"Hypocrite," she snarls. "You *placed* that ad, looking for an anonymous sex partner!"

"*I'm* not a virgin!"

"Watch it, Trevor," I warn him. "You have *no right* to judge me!"

"I'm not judging you," I say, taking a deep breath and trying to calm myself down. "I'm just…surprised."

"Stop acting like a prissy schoolmarm from the last century. We're both adults."

"But I…" I'm about to say, *"I thought you were better than this,"* but I stop myself in time. There are some comments you can come back from. I'm not sure that would be one of them. Again, I mumble, "I'm just…surprised."

"Talk about a double standard," she says, crossing her arms over her chest, which has the effect of drawing my eyes to her breasts, which are plump and full under a flimsy white top.

I step back and look at her again—at her heels and designer jeans, the gold accents in her outfit and the way her breasts almost spill out of the V in her shirt. Not to mention her wild hair and sexy makeup. She looks hot as hell, and yet I can't seem to tamp down the overwhelming need to grab my overcoat from the closet by the front entrance and throw it over her.

"Why are you dressed like this?" I ask.

"Like the picture of Faith Crawford?" she asks. "So you'd recognize me, of course."

"Was that picture even of you?"

Her jaw drops. "Of course it was. No one's trying to *put one over* on you, Trevor!"

"Where was it taken?"

"Off the coast of Nantucket, sailing with my sister, whose clothes I was wearing in the photo."

"Well, it's *not* what you normally look like," I say, crossing my arms over my chest to mirror her.

"Not that you minded...before you realized it was me."

"What's that supposed to mean?"

"I saw your face, T. I saw your eyes. You *liked* what you saw when I walked into this room."

She's right. I did. And part of me feels bad about that...feels *guilty*.

"I'm—I was *confused*!" I yell. "I'm still confused! Hell! Are you wild and free Faith Crawford or uptight virgin Faye Findley?"

She gasps, recoiling from me. "You're a bastard."

"No, baby. I'm just playing catchup."

"Don't call me 'baby,'" she hisses, blinking her eyes furiously as she shakes her head. "And don't lie—you're pissed off at me because I wanted the exact same thing you did: easy, meaningless sex with someone over New Year's weekend, so I wouldn't feel so goddamned lonely over the worst holiday of the year."

I lift my chin. "It didn't feel like the worst this morning. It felt pretty awesome."

"And it doesn't now?" she asks me, her eyes glassy. "I'm still...*me*, Trevor." She looks over her shoulder at the hotel entrance, then takes off her sunglasses and pushes a hand through her hair. "You know what? I need some air."

"You're in Alaska," I say, gesturing toward the door. "There's plenty!"

She turns around and starts walking away from me, her sexy shoes clacking over the shiny black marble as she heads to the French doors that lead outside. I watch her go, taking in her long legs, rounded ass, and trim waist in tight denim. Her dark hair, with red highlights caught by the fire's glow, tumbles down her back in messy waves that I'm dying to touch. I want to twist my hand in that hair, winding it around my hand as I thrust into her, making her moan and whimper.

For a second, I feel bad that I'm lusting after her, but then remind myself that she *is*, in fact, the same woman I've been falling for over the last few days. I'm not betraying Faye by desiring Faith.

They're the same person, you jackass. Innocent *and* sexy. Fun *and* smart. Ambitious *and* adorable.

The doors open automatically, and she whooshes through them without looking back. Suddenly, I'm left alone in the posh, modern lobby, wishing she'd come back, longing to get to know this other side of Faye. I glance at the desk attendant who side-eyes me, shaking her head in disdain.

I'm going to go after her. I just need a second to think. I need to understand this.

Honestly, I should be happy, right? Out of the slew of women who answered the ad, I *chose* Faith Cra—Faye Findley. She was my one percent. And as I piece it all together, it makes sense:

Her polite, business-like tone and perfect English appealed to me…and still do.

The woman in the picture I received is beautiful…and I think whether Faye comes to dinner in a demure sweater dress or shows up in the lobby of a hotel in tight jeans and a low-cut blouse, she's crazy beautiful.

I wanted to have amazing sex with a willing partner over New Year's, and God knows I still do, but now I have *feelings* for that woman too. Even better.

I may have fallen for Faith Crawford virtually, but I fell for Faye Findley in person, and in a shocking twist, it turns out I can actually have both.

So why am I acting like a total asshole?

Crushing the rose I dropped on the floor as I hurry to the front door, I step quickly through it, looking left and right for any sign of Faye.

"Fuck," I mutter, turning to the doorman, who's dressed in a heavy overcoat. "The woman who just came out…where did she go?"

"That way," he says, gesturing to a lighted path to the left of the building.

As I round the corner of the building, I see Faye

standing in the moonlight. No coat. Arms crossed over her chest. She's staring at the white-covered mountains in the distance with her back to me, and my heart fists because she looks so fucking beautiful, and I've yelled at her and made her feel bad for no good reason.

"Faye," I call to her.

She twists at the waist to face me, but as she does, something happens to her balance. I watch in horror as her arms spring outward to steady her, but she's too late. She's already slipping, her high heels trying to find traction but unable, and she falls onto the icy snow with a strangled cry.

"Faye!"

I race to her side, kneeling beside her in the snow.

"My foot! Oh, my God, Trevor. My foot. I heard it crack!"

She's lying on her side, panting and sobbing, and my eyes trail quickly down her leg. Her feet don't look injured, but that doesn't mean they aren't.

"H-help," she whimpers, trying to sit up, but her hands are bare, and her clothes are getting soaked in the snow.

"Stop moving," I tell her. "Let me get your shoe off and look at it, okay?"

"Trevor," she sobs. "Help."

"I will, sweetheart."

I reach for the strap on her shoe, intending to unbuckle it, but she wails in pain, wildly grabbing at my arm.

"Noooo! Stop! P-Please stop. Don't t-touch it."

"If you heard it crack, I think it's broken," I tell her, looking at her face, which is screwed up in pain, with tears glistening on her cheek, streaking her dark eye makeup. I reach forward and use my thumbs to swipe her cheeks dry.

"M-Me too," she pants.

"I need to get you to the hospital. If I pick you up, can you loop your arms around my neck?"

"I…think so."

"It's going to hurt," I tell her, "when I pick you up. But I've got to get you into my car."

"I can handle it," she says, clenching her jaw.

Sliding my arms under her knees and behind her back, I left her as gently as I can, ignoring her cry of pain as her ankle lifts off the ground and swings awkwardly as I gather her into my arms.

She wraps her arms around my neck but keeps her own neck stiff as I walk slowly back down the path to the front door. The doorman sees us coming and rushes forward.

"Bring my car around! She's hurt!"

"Should I call an ambulance?"

"It'll be faster if I drive her. Get my car. Now!"

As he hustles toward a garage to the right of the main building, I readjust my arms around Faith, holding her closer. "Are you cold?"

"It hurts like crazy," she says. "Too much to notice anything else."

She's stopped crying now and her face is stoic, though she certainly has the right to be sobbing in pain. "I'm sorry, Faye. For before."

"Trevor, I can't…" She takes a deep breath. "I can't focus on that right now."

"Sorry. I understand," I tell her, relieved when the doorman arrives with my car. He opens the back door, and as gently as possible, I slide Faye into the back seat.

"Your coat, sir?" he asks. "Her things?"

"I'll come back," I tell him. "Thanks for your help."

I jump in the driver's seat, and drive, as quickly as I can, to get help for Faye.

CHAPTER TEN

Trevor

I arrive at the hospital twenty minutes later, screech to a halt in front of the emergency room doors, and tell Faye to hold tight for a second while I get help.

Striding through the electronic doors, I approach the receptionist. I'm not going to let them make Faye wait. She's getting in right away, even if I need to play up her injuries a little to get her immediate care.

"I have an injured woman in my car."

She jumps up from her desk, looking over my shoulder. "What happened?"

"Broken bones. Hurry!"

Now, I know as well as any other Alaskan that broken bones can mean a bear attack, a bar fight, or a slip on some ice, but I let her think the worst and watch as she picks up her phone, dials three numbers, and orders a gurney to the ER entrance.

Satisfied that Faye will be met with expedited service, I race back outside to stay with her until the orderlies arrive.

When I open the backdoor of my car, she's sitting up.

"Someone's coming," I tell her.

"It hurts like hell."

"I'm sorry about that."

"Sure you are." She purses her lips and looks away from me.

"Of course I am, Faye! I care about you."

"Oh really? You care about a *slut wannabe with no self-respect who somehow tricked you into meeting her*? Give me a break. I know *exactly* how you feel about me."

"Whoa. You're…pissed."

"Does that surprise you?" Her eyes snap back to grab mine. "You were a *total* asshole to me back there, T."

"I was…shocked. It never occurred to me that you and Faith were the same person."

"Well, it never occurred to me that you and Mr. Fairbanks were the same person."

"I've had a tough year where betrayal is concerned. I think I went into some sort of self-protection mode." I run a hand through my hair. "I was caught off guard, Faye. I just needed to get my head around it, and once I did, I came outside to find you."

I still want to ask her why she'd arrange to sleep with a man—*give her virginity to man*—she didn't even know, but I have a strong feeling that would add gasoline to this fire.

As she processes my words, her face starts to soften, but suddenly, the ER doors open, and two men run outside with a gurney, placing it beside my car.

"Back away, please, sir. We'll handle it from here."

I watch as they help her out of the back seat of my car and onto the gurney, wheeling her quickly into the hospital. I follow behind, but a nurse stops me as they take Faye back to the examination area.

"I'm sorry, sir. You can't just…"

Her hand is flat on my chest, but I haven't glanced at her face because I'm too busy watching Faye. Finally, I look down at her and…

Holy shit.

Marlena.

"Trevor," she whispers, yanking her hand away.

"Marlena," I say softly, looking into her blue eyes for the first time since June. I take a deep breath, looking over her head to see Faye wheeled into a curtained-off area, then back at my ex-fiancée. "I need to go with her."

Marlena shifts her body so she's standing in front of me, blocking my way.

"Um…I'm sorry, Trevor…you can't come back here without permission."

"I *brought* her here."

"That's great," she says, "because she obviously needs help. She also needs to give her permission for you to stay with her while she receives treatment."

"Please go ask her for permission."

"There's a form you need to—fine. I'll ask."

She turns on her heel and walks swiftly to the area where Faye is concealed, speaking with someone behind the curtain for a moment before returning to me.

"She says…" Marlena sighs loudly, looking away from me.

"What?"

"She says you're welcome to join her if you're finished

acting like a horse's ass."

I can't help it. I whoop with laughter. Loudly. Even…joyfully.

"Tell her I'm finished."

"Oh…just go," she says, gesturing to the trauma bay, where a doctor in a white coat pulls the curtain aside.

My eyes skim back to Marlena, who's still standing in front of me in peach-colored scrubs, and for the first time, I realize that her belly is sticking out a little. I stare at it for a second before sliding my eyes to her face. Somehow, the face that I once thought was my "forever" doesn't hold the same promise or allure. She's just a pretty girl who's going to have a baby.

"Congratulations."

Her cheeks color, and she licks her lips before looking at her white sneakers. "Trev, we never meant—"

"—to hurt me. I know." I glance over to the curtained area where the doctor is still consulting and then back at the mother of my niece. "The reality is that we weren't a good match. I didn't know it at the time, but we…weren't."

"I know," she says, her face surprised, then soft. "I knew it for a long time."

"You could have told me."

"Could I?" she asks.

I blink at her, then shake my head. "Maybe not. I don't know."

"You're…Trevor. The oldest. The most ambitious. The go-getter. I wasn't…I mean, I didn't…"

I clear my throat. "We weren't right for each other.

That's all there is to it."

She searches my face like she wants to say something else, but I don't want to talk to Marlena anymore. I want to see if Faye's okay. As I start to walk away, however, my ex-fiancée grabs my sleeve. I turn around to find her looking at me intently.

"Forgive Cecil," she says. "Please forgive him. He can't—he can't live without you, Trevor."

Gently, I pull my arm away, tilting my head to the side. "Probably should have thought of that before he fu—ahem, before you two got together."

She nods once, then takes a deep breath, blinking her eyes. "You have no idea how much he misses you, how much he loves you."

I shrug my shoulders.

"Please, Trevor," she begs me. "For Aurora."

My eyes skim down to her belly again, and I process her request. Aurora. Aurora is a person growing inside of Marlena. My niece. My family. She could be born with my eyes or my mother's smile or my father's weird way of laughing. She's part of my family, this Aurora, even though she isn't even here yet.

"I'll see what I can do," I mutter. "Now, leave it."

"Thanks," she whispers. "Trauma bay six…and Trev? The girl with the broken foot? I like her."

Not that I require Marlena's approval, but I find myself grinning at her before walking quickly over to Faye's bedside.

Me too.

***

"I'm sorry, Ms. Findley," says the doctor two hours later. "But the X-rays are conclusive. You have an avulsion fracture of the proximal fifth metatarsal."

"Layman's terms, please?" Faye asks.

"You broke your foot. We need to set it, then cast it or boot it."

I'm in a chair beside her, where I've been sitting since she returned from radiation twenty minutes ago. "What do you recommend?"

"The boot," he says, "as long as you only take it off for showering and don't try to walk around for at least six weeks, but probably closer to eight."

"Six to eight weeks!" Faye exclaims. "What about the bathroom? What about work?"

"Yes, you can go to the bathroom with crutches, and yes, you can take off the boot to shower. No, you cannot go back to the office yet, but luckily, we live in the internet age."

"Work remotely?" she asks, her voice hushed and shocked.

"Is your office nearby?" he asks.

"Only if you consider Boston local."

He chuckles. "Oh, Ms. Findley, you're a hoot."

"So that's a no?" she asks.

"That's a *hell no*," says the doctor. "The injury aside, that's a long flight, which could lead to edema. You can fly back to Massachusetts on"—he looks at his watch—"or around Valentine's Day. Until then, welcome to Fairbanks! You'll need to stay put. Now, I'm going to go arrange for a boot. You sit tight."

"Six weeks," she laments, looking up at me. "But I'm supposed to be home on January second!"

"You heard the doc," I say.

"But…but I can't just stay here."

"Yes, you can," I tell her, reaching for her hand. "You'll stay with me."

She whips her neck around to face me, her eyes wide. "I can't…no! I can't *stay* with you. No. You don't even like me anymore and besides—"

"I like you better than anyone else," I tell her, "so there is no 'besides.' You'll be my guest until you get the doc's okay to go home. Deal?"

"I already have a room at the Chalet Blanche. I'm sure they can extend my reservation until—"

"Faye," I say, lacing my fingers through hers. "Look at me." I clear my throat. "I would like to invite you to be my guest for the month of January and half of February. I have plenty of space in my home, and I want you to stay with me."

"Three hours ago," she says, trying to pull her hand away from mine, "you were pretty nasty to me."

"Sweetheart," I say, unlacing our fingers but still holding her hand. "I am *not* smooth. I am sometimes an asshole, yes, but I promise you, I don't *mean* to be." I rub her hand in mine, lifting it to my lips before lowering it again. "I was surprised. I was caught off guard. I was—oh fuck—I was *attracted* to Faith and that felt like *cheating* on Faye and cheating is…is…"

"That's ridiculous," she says. "Faith and Faye are the same person. Me!"

"I've had a weird year where cheating's concerned," I tell her. "Cut me some slack, huh?"

She inclines her head just a touch, then says, "*You* placed the ad, but you acted all shocked and bothered that I answered it. Why?"

This is a tougher question, because the honest answer is that I'm probably a little sexist, which is totally and completely unfair. I have no right to judge her for something I was also willing to do. But…she's a virgin.

"Didn't you want your first time to be special?" I ask her.

"When I answered your ad?" Her shoulders slump. "No, actually. I just wanted to get it over with." She takes a deep breath and exhales. "I had no prospects, no boyfriend, no special feelings for anyone. I thought…well, I thought I'd come up here and just…you know…have fun…see what all the fuss is about…jump-start my love life…"

"By having sex with a total stranger."

"Yes," she says, locking her eyes with mine. "Same as you."

"But you changed your mind?"

"Of course," she says. "I wouldn't have agreed to spend New Year's with *you* if I hadn't."

"Why'd you change your mind?"

I'm ninety-nine percent sure I know the answer to this question, but I need to hear it. I need to know.

Her lips tilt up in a gentle smile as she reaches forward

to cup my cheek with her free hand. "Because I met you, T. Because after I met you…I didn't—didn't want anyone else to be my first. I want *you*. That's all I know."

I tilt my face so I can kiss her palm. "I want you too."

She wets her lips. "Did we just make up?"

I nod slowly. "I think we did."

"And you're sure you don't mind a long-term houseguest?" she asks me.

"I wouldn't have it any other way."

***

Carrying Faye from my car up to my bedroom is the easiest work I've ever done.

She leans her weary cheek against my shoulder, and her curls, which only seem wilder after our crazy evening together, tickle my throat. Still clad only in her underwear, a hospital gown and a coat borrowed from the hospital Lost & Found, I lay her gently on my bed in the moonlight.

"Give me a second," I say. "I'll turn down the covers on the other side and get you a T-shirt to wear."

She leans up on her elbows. "I hate to be so much trouble. I could stay at the Chalet Bl—"

"You're staying here," I tell her, my voice firm and brooking no dissent. "That's final."

"Thank you, Trevor," she whispers, lying back.

I turn on the light in my bathroom to add some ambient light to the room, then rifle through my top bureau drawer for a T-shirt. I choose one that reads, "My Compass Points North" over the logo of North Star Spirits and hand it to her. Then I fish the vial of hospital-prescribed painkillers out of my pocket and put it on the bedside table next to my water bottle.

"Do you need help?" I ask. "With your clothes?"

"No," she says, looking up at me from my pillow. "But maybe a little privacy?"

"Fuck," I say, jumping a step backward. "Yeah. Yeah. Of course. Sorry."

"It's okay," she says, her voice tired but slightly amused.

"I'll be right downstairs," I tell her. "What can I get you? Vodka? Gin?"

"Tea?" she asks, her voice dipping a little. "My mother used to make me tea when I was sick."

"I don't know what I have," I warn her, "but I promise I'll...find something."

As I stride to the open door, she calls after me, "Come back, T."

"Right now?"

She chuckles softly in the dark. "No. Just...come back. I'm...I don't want to be alone."

"I'll be back with your tea," I say, praying I have at least one tea bag somewhere in this house and closing my bedroom door behind me.

For a second or two, I lean against the closed door in the hallway, closing my eyes and taking a deep breath. With Faye safely in my bed, about to get a good night's sleep she sorely needs, it's the first easy breath I've taken in about five hours. I think about our fight in the lobby of the Chalet Blanche, the sound of her cries when she broke her foot, seeing Marlena's face in the ER, and making up with Faye after her X-rays…and my heart…fuck, my heart…hurts. Or finally doesn't hurt. I don't know. I just *feel* so much, and it's almost entirely focused on the woman in my bed, who is going to be my guest for the next six weeks or so.

And it's that thought that makes my eyes open and my lips tilt up in a smile.

For the next six weeks, Faye Findley is all mine.

Frankly, I can't think of anything I'd like better.

I hurry downstairs to the kitchen, where I comb my cabinets for a tea bag, finally finding Yerba Mate in the back of my aluminum foil drawer, no doubt put there by Inez and enjoyed while she's working.

I heat up a mug of water in the microwave and put a tea bag in the hot water, letting it steep for a minute or two while I lean against the counter.

You could throw a dart at tonight and hit twenty crazy occurrences, but the craziest of all to me wasn't actually when I realized that Faye and Faith were the same person…it was realizing that my feelings for Marlena are absolutely, positively over. I was surprised to see her, of course, but it didn't hurt my heart or make it soar. It just…was. *Oh, here's my ex, Marlena, the nurse, to help my injured girlfriend, Faye.*

I jerk away from the counter as I realize that I called Faye my "girlfriend" in my head.

My girlfriend…*mine.*

It's far from the truth because we're still getting to know each other, and yet people who meet during extreme or extraordinary circumstances often find themselves moving faster than those who evolve from friendship to romance or date for ages before declaring a commitment.

And the reality is…between the ad I placed and our pen names as Mr. Fairbanks and Faith Crawford, in addition to the way we met by chance on Christmas Eve and spent Christmas Day together, only to realize we knew of one another in real life, and ended up spending the next two days together…it *has been* extraordinary. Somehow Faye Findley and I have packed months' worth of circumstances, emotions, and coincidences into a five-day meeting. It's sped up everything. I haven't even processed all of it yet.

Throwing the tea bag in the sink, I head back upstairs and tiptoe into my room, gingerly placing the mug on the bedside table next to Faye, who somehow managed to wiggle under the covers with her boot on. Because she's meant to keep it elevated, I steal two pillows from the guest room across the hall, and lift the covers of my bed to place them under her foot. Unfortunately, I wake her up as I'm holding her bare leg in my hands.

"T?" she murmurs.

"I'm here, sweetheart," I say, finishing my work, covering her up, then squatting down beside her so my face is closer to hers. "I just wanted to get your leg elevated."

She sniffles softly. "I broke my foot."

"You did," I say.

"I can't go home for six weeks."

"I know."

"It h-hurts," she half-sighs, half-sobs.

"Did you take a painkiller? I left them—"

"I did," she says, sniffling again. "It hasn't kicked in yet."

"It will," I say, brushing the hair from her forehead. "Soon."

"Will you...will you lie down?" she asks. "Next to me?"

"Yeah. Of course," I whisper, standing up and pulling off my suit jacket.

I grab some sweats and another T-shirt from my bureau and take them into the bathroom. I throw my pants, shirt, undershirt, and socks in the hamper and quickly change. When I come out, her breathing is deep and easy, and I think she's asleep until I slip under the covers beside her.

"I need to be sure you know," she says, turning her head to face me, "that I only walked into that lobby tonight to tell Mr. Fairbanks that I'd met someone else. I was going to call the whole deal off. I have a check in my purse that I was going to offer him to cover his expenses."

I slide my hand across the bottom sheet to find hers. Once I do, I lace our fingers together.

"I know," I say. "I was there to do exactly the same: to tell Faith Crawford that I'd met someone else with whom I wanted to share my New Year's."

"Lucky you," she deadpans. "Now you get to spend the entire month of January and half of February with her too."

I squeeze her hand, then lift it to my lips and kiss her knuckles, one at a time, each in turn.

"Lucky me," I whisper into the darkness. "Lucky fucking bastard that I get more time with you."

She chuckles softly. "Maybe I broke my foot on

purpose so we wouldn't have to say good-bye yet."

"If you did, that's completely brilliant. You knew what I wanted even before I did."

"Thank you for letting me stay...for taking care of me," she says.

I scooch closer to her, until our hips are side by side and touching. Then I lower our joined hands to my chest and rest them over my heart.

"Thanks for breaking your foot," I say. "Now get some sleep, sweetheart."

***

Faye

Despite the weariness of my body, it took a while for me to fall asleep in someone else's bed.

I don't know how late it was when I finally drifted off, but I had to go to the bathroom around three and woke up Trevor by mistake when one of my crutches crashed to the ground. He insisted on carrying me to the bathroom, but pulling down my underwear proved challenging, and standing up from the toilet made sharp darts of pain shoot up my leg. I called to him when I was finished but forgot to flush the toilet, which bothered me for over an hour before I gave up worrying about it and finally went back to sleep.

My eyes open and focus, staring first at the ceiling, then to my right, alerted to T's presence by the light tap of fingers on a keyboard. He's sitting up beside me with an open laptop, which—for no good reason—makes me happy.

I clear my raspy throat. "'Morning."

He stops typing and slides his eyes to me. "Hey...look

who's awake!"

I try to sit up, but my foot immediately protests, screaming in pain, and my bladder, which hasn't been emptied in nine hours, sloshes around, full again.

"Ohhhh, fuck. I'm a mess."

"What?" he asks, putting his laptop aside and jumping up. "What do you need?"

I look up at him, my eyes filling with tears, feeling so goddamned helpless, it's pathetic.

"I need to pee…I'm thirsty and hungry…my foot is *killing* me…"

He squats down beside me, opens the vial of pills beside the bed, takes out one, and hands it to me with a bottle of water. "For the pain."

I swallow it down gratefully, chugging the rest of the water in the bottle because I'm so thirsty.

Trevor stands up. "Ready for the bathroom?"

I nod, reaching my arms up to him. He pulls off the covers and scoops me up, opening the toilet seat with his foot and settling me gently on top. "Call me when you're done."

"Thank you," I murmur, sniffling pathetically as he closes the door.

I plant my good foot on the floor, lean up, and yank at my panties. One side gets caught between my thigh and the seat, but I finally manage to pull them down enough to pee, all the while letting my tears flow freely.

In my entire life, I don't think I've ever felt this helpless or this pitiful. I mean, I own a massive company, a huge house, two cars, and my bank accounts have millions, but I can't even get to the bathroom on my own. This situation is…humiliating…and humbling…and a little terrifying too.

I need to get on my phone or laptop and explain to Carlene and the board that I won't be back in Boston until mid-February. Except I don't even have a laptop with me. All my stuff, including my phone, is at the Chalet Blanche.

My steady trickle of tears turns into full-blown sobs that echo loudly in the tiled bathroom and you know what? I don't care. I don't. I let it out. I let it *all* out. The pain. The helplessness. Everything.

"Faye? Faye, are you okay?"

I continue to weep loudly, shaking my head back and forth, *no*, even though he can't see me.

"Faye, did you fall? What's going on?"

I didn't fall. My life is in shambles.

"Faye, if you don't answer, I'm coming in."

"I'm…on…the…t-toilet! Stay out!"

"Why are you crying?"

"Because…I'm…a…m-mess!" I sob through a deluge a fresh tears. I pull some toilet paper from the roll and blow my snotty nose.

"Well, if you finish up in there, I'll come and get you, and we can talk. I can help. I promise."

I don't want to talk, I think, feeling very, very sorry for myself.

"Faye?" he prompts. "I called the Chalet Blanche, explained what happened, and they said my brother could go pick up your things as soon as you called them yourself to release the room and your things."

This appeals to me because, although it's a tiny step, at least it's a plan to address one of my current woes: getting my stuff.

"O-Okay," I say. "C-Can I b-borrow your ph-phone? I'll c-call them."

"You know," he says, "my brother, Cez, broke his foot when he was sixteen. Same kind of fracture as yours. He was playing ice frisbee and slipped. Anyway. He was in bed for a couple of days, but my dad found him an office chair...you know...with casters? And he could roll around from room to room, and it gave him a lot more freedom. I have an office chair downstairs. I could bring it up and you could use it to get around."

Actually? That sounds amazing. So much better than relying on Trevor to carry me everywhere.

"Um...I don't know if you remember, but across the hall from my room, there's a guest room. It has a bed and bathroom, but it also has a desk area. I was thinking you could use it if you wanted to."

Two thoughts immediately pop into my head.

The first is *Awesome. I'll be able to get some work done.*

The second is *He doesn't want me in his bed. One night with me was more than enou—*

"I mean..." He clears his throat. "You can use the room for *work*. Not the bed. Sleep in *my* bed...with *me*...okay?"

For the first time since I started crying, a small smile blooms across my face, because I'm so relieved that he's not trying to get rid of me.

"Yes," I say, taking a jagged breath and sighing. "Thank you. All of that sounds…really good. Thank you, Trevor."

I tear some extra toilet paper from the roll, wipe myself, and stand up on one foot. After I pull up my underwear, I hop to the sink and use the bar of soap in the saucer to wash my face and hands. My hair is a wild tangle, so I quickly French-braid it, hoping it will hold because I don't have an elastic. Then I hop to the door and open it.

Trevor is sitting on the floor, leaning against the doorway, and looks up at me.

"There you are," he says.

"Here I am."

His eyes skim up my leg, and I realize I'm standing over him in nothing but an orthopedic boot, panties, and a T-shirt. I've never been this naked in front of a man who wasn't my doctor, and it makes me blush.

"Looking good," he says, his lips turning up as his eyes find mine.

"You're a flirt."

He pushes off from the floor and stands up slowly, holding my eyes the whole time. When he's standing at his full height, I have to tilt my neck back a little because he's six or seven inches taller than me.

"I'm just being honest. You look good in my T-shirt…and not much else."

"Thank you," I whisper.

His hand, which had been dangling by his hip, rises to rest on my left jaw and cheek, gently cupping my face.

"You're welcome."

With infinite tenderness, he lowers his head, brushing his lips across mine. My eyes close, my upturned face straining to meet his, my arms reaching up to loop around his neck. There are short, bristly hairs back there that tickle my fingertips as he kisses me. His tongue sweeps slowly across my lips but doesn't slide into my mouth.

Without any warning, he lifts me into his arms like I weigh nothing, still nipping at my lips, first the top, then the bottom. He grazes and pecks, brushes and teases, his breath warm and soft as it slips between my lips to mingle with mine.

When he lowers me back to the bed, our lips part, and when my eyes open, I find him hovering over me, his beautiful face scanning mine with wonder.

"I'm falling for you hard, Faye," he says, his voice a soft rumble, his eyes worried and tender at once.

In a flash of awareness, I remember what Marlena did to him, and I realize he needs me to reassure him, to comfort him, to let him know that—

"You're not alone," I say, reaching up to caress his bristly cheek the same way he did to me. "I'm falling for you too."

He rotates his neck just enough to kiss my palm, then sighs, offering me a small, relieved smile. "Okay, sweetheart. You peed. You had a painkiller and water. How about something to eat?"

On cue, my stomach rumbles, and I drop my hand, placing it over my belly. "Yes, please."

"Toast and eggs?"

"Heaven," I tell him.

He leans down and kisses my forehead, pausing for a moment before straightening up again. "You're not alone either. I'm here for you. Whatever you need."

I smile up at him, holding back my tears until he leaves the room and I can hear his footfalls on the stairs leading downstairs.

And then I lean back on pillows that smell like Trevor, and I weep a little more…not because I feel sorry for myself, but because my heart brims with a tenderness I've never known before now.

***

Two days later, I don't know how much my foot has improved, but I've got the pain under control with a combination of Advil and Tylenol every six hours, and my prescription painkillers every twelve. Hopping, using the crutches, or wheeling myself around on Trevor's old office chair, I can get to the bathroom or across the hallway to my makeshift office.

I talked to Harry yesterday, explaining what happened and telling her that I'd no longer be in Boston next week.

Her reaction surprised me:

"Then I'll come and see you in Fairbanks instead."

"No, Harry," I said. "It's too far, and—"

"It's not too far, and I don't have to be back at school for two more weeks. I want to come and see you for a few days. If you say no, I'll use my credit card and buy a ticket anyway, so you may as well agree, Faye."

Touched by her insistence, I had Carlene book her a ticket to Fairbanks, with a stopover in Seattle on the way home so that she can meet Karl and be the face of Findley Imports at the UNNW meeting on January seventh.

At first, Harry said that she wasn't ready for so much responsibility, but I assured her that Karl would take care of the negotiations. I just felt it was important for there to be a Findley present at the meeting, since, if it goes the way I hope, it will be a historic merger. Once I'd promised her that she was more of an observer than anything else, she seemed to get excited about the opportunity to see how our business works; plus, I'll take some time while she's visiting Fairbanks to coach her through what to expect.

What I am learning, more than anything, is that dependence and delegation will be unavoidable over the next six weeks, and the sooner I embrace both and work within their frameworks and limitations, the better it will be for me and for my company.

To that end, I have already promoted Karl Franklin to interim-CEO of Findley Imports, though I maintain my position as president. Knowing that my company rests in Karl's loyal and capable hands is allowing me to breathe easier and cope more gracefully with my convalescence.

Sitting at the desk in Trevor's guest room, I write an emailed letter to the board, letting them know that Karl will be my voice over the next six to eight weeks and that they should regard his decisions as my own.

Ding. Ding. Ding. Ding.

At six o'clock, the alarm on my watch dings to tell me

to get ready for Trevor's and my New Year's Eve celebration. This morning, he told me he'd be carrying me downstairs at seven o'clock for a champagne dinner and that neither my laptop nor my phone were invited.

I close my laptop and use my hands to push away from the desk, wheeling myself into the guest room bathroom, which I have taken over. Holding on to the robe hook next to the shower, I undress on one foot, then sit on the side of the tub to unbuckle my boot. As carefully as I can, I remove it, maneuver my body into the shower, and stand on one foot as I shower for the first time since Friday.

Lord, it feels…good.

As I soap my body and delight in the hot water sluicing down my aching muscles, I think about everything Trevor has done for me over the past two days.

By welcoming me into his home, helping me acclimate to the limitations of my injured body, making our meals and sitting beside me in his bed at night as we work side by side on our laptops, he's given me a glimpse into the life I could have with him. And I find—more and more—that it's the *only* life I can see for myself. The only life I *want* for myself. Day by day, my longing is deeper and stronger, my feelings growing at a breakneck speed as he continues to prove to me that he could be—no…*is*—everything I want for the rest of my life.

Although there is one area of our relationship that is yet untested.

Though our comfort with one another and sense of intimacy increases daily, our physical relationship has not advanced with the same swiftness as our emotional connection.

It's not lost on me that in the original iteration of my New Year's plans, I would've lost my virginity to a stranger by now. Instead, because of circumstances beyond my control, I'm on the verge of falling in love with Trevor Starling, though we have barely progressed beyond kissing.

The strangest thing of all, however, is the fact that I no longer think of my virginity as something to "get rid of" but as something I will willingly give to a man I respect and trust—a man for whom I have vibrantly alive, constantly deepening feelings that are rooted in a foundation I didn't know we were building until I felt the beautiful bright-green tendrils of affection, of tenderness, of longing, bursting through the dark ground and reaching heavenward to the bright sun of his love.

CHAPTER ELEVEN

Trevor

On January third, I arrange for Inez to stay the day at my house so I can go to the offices of North Star Spirits without worrying about Faye.

Good intentions aside, however, I'm getting absolutely nothing done.

My mind is full of her: her touch, her scent, the sounds she makes when I'm kissing her, when I'm touching her, when she orgasms—

I blink at my computer screen, filling my lungs with a deep breath and forcing myself to calm down, but the memories linger and my dick strains against the zipper of my jeans.

We almost had sex on New Year's Eve.

Wait. Let me back up.

When I went upstairs at seven o'clock, she was sitting on the edge of the bed, waiting for me. I knew she'd taken a shower because her hair, tumbling freely around her shoulders, was still damp. And instead of my T-shirt and panties, she was wearing these flimsy little shorts with flowers on them, a white V-neck T-shirt and a loose-fitting, fuzzy blue sweat shirt.

My eyes shot to the shorts, then skimmed up to her face.

"The boot makes pants tough." She shrugged, giving me a little smile. "I didn't bring any shorts to Alaska, except these. They're pajama bottoms."

I nodded, wishing she was wearing the top too, which I assumed was just as flimsy.

"Ready for New Year's Eve?" I asked her.

She raised her arms, and I scooped her into mine, breathing in the scent of her shampoo and shower gel, and reveling in the comfortable weight of her body as I carried her down the stairs, brimming with anticipation. I'd spent hours this afternoon preparing for tonight.

As we got to the bottom of the stairs, where the living room was in full view, I heard her gasp softly, and in that moment, all my hard work was worth it.

"Trevor!" She sighed. "It's so beautiful!"

I'd roped white lights on the rafters, and there was a fire roaring in the fireplace. But on every surface, including the table set for two, were votive candles, flicking with soft white light, and making the whole room magical.

"Happy New Year's Eve, sweetheart," I said, waiting for her eyes as they scanned the room before returning to me. "Mr. Fairbanks promised a night to remember, so…"

"You're amazing, Trevor."

With her arms still looped around my neck, she pulled my face closer to hers and pressed her lips to mine, sweeping her tongue inside of my mouth with a low moan. Kissing her back, I crossed the room and lowered myself to the couch with Faye still in my arms, cradled on my lap.

Go slow, I told myself. *Let her be in charge.*

Her fingers wound through my hair, and she turned slightly in my arms, pressing her chest to mine, wiggling to get closer to me, her breathing shallow and erratic. One of my hands slipped beneath her shirt and sweat shirt, flattening on the smooth, warm plane of her stomach. She gasped softly, then arched her back, inviting me to touch her further.

As we kissed, my hand skimmed upward, trailing over the curves of her ribs to the soft flesh beneath her breasts. And that's when I realized she wasn't wearing a bra. Her breasts, perfect handfuls of warm, silky flesh, were unbound, waiting to be touched, maybe for the first time.

I gently caressed them with the back of my hand, feeling the tight pucker of her nipples and encouraged by her sharp intake of breath. Carefully, reminding myself that this precious woman may not have ever been in a position this intimate, this vulnerable, before now, I covered one breast with the palm of my hand. Squeezing and kneading gently, my mouth watered, hungry to take those stiff points of flesh between my mouth and love them the same way I was kissing her lips, with nips and tugs, gentle bites and licks.

Breaking our kiss and dragging my hand away from her breast, I picked her up, then laid her back down on the couch, careful to elevate her boot on the arm.

"Trust me?" I asked.

Her eyes, dark and drunk with desire, looked up at me. "Implicitly."

I knelt beside her, pushing up her shirt and sweat shirt until her beautiful breasts were bared to me, the light-pink areolas circling darker-pink nipples.

"*Fuck*," I sighed. "You're gorgeous."

Her smile was small and trusting. "If you say so."

"I do," I said, leaning my head down to take one puckered nub between my lips.

Licking and sucking the tight bud gently, I felt myself getting hard as she strained under my touch, tiny whimpers and moans slipping from her lips as I skimmed my own over her skin to take the other nipple into my mouth.

"Teeeeee," she sighed, plunging her hands into my hair. She pulled and twisted the strands, which hurt but also turned me on. My other hand slid down her chest, over her belly, and under the waistband of her shorts.

I leaned up from her breasts as my fingers touched down on a small, neat patch of hair.

"Is this…okay?" I asked, my voice rough and raspy.

"Mm-hm," she murmured, digging the back of her head into the couch cushion as my fingers glided into her slickened folds to find her clit.

She whimpered with pleasure, her pelvis pushing upward slightly to meet my touch. With one hand, I caressed her breast, and with the other, I rubbed tiny circles around the erect button of her sex, listening for the sounds of her moans and whimpers, which became faster and louder until her body seized under my fingers, and she cried out my name, "T-Trevor!"

As she rode out the waves of her orgasm with eyes

closed, I leaned up to kiss her. She panted into my mouth, moaning softly with aftershocks, and when her eyes finally opened, looking up at me, I felt like a fucking god.

"Wow," she murmured.

"Good?" I asked, pulling her shirt back down over her breasts.

"*So* good," she hummed, reaching for my face and looking into my eyes. "But I want more."

Fuck. Were sweeter words ever uttered?

"More…*how*?"

"More…*everything*." She bit her bottom lip, still staring up at me. "I want to have sex with you. I want you to…make love to me."

My heart.

I didn't think my heart would ever fall in love again.

I thought—after Marlena and Cez betrayed me—that true love simply wasn't in the cards for me. What I didn't know, was that I just hadn't met the right woman yet. But then I knew, in the depths of my soul, that the plan was never for me to be with Marlena. All along, I was meant for Faye.

"I…" I swallowed. *My feelings for you are so strong*, I thought. *I want your first time to be perfect. I want you to be sure.* "We don't have to rush."

She leaned up on one elbow, her brows creased. "You don't want to?"

"Sweetheart," I said. "I'm *dying* to."

I sat down on the couch beside her and took her hand, pressing it over the zipper of my jeans so she could feel my hard, straining cock.

Her cheeks colored, but she didn't move her hand away.

"Then…"

Raising her hand to my lips and kissing it, I looked deeply into her eyes. "There's no rush. We have time."

"I know that. But I want—"

"I need you to be sure," I said, and suddenly I realized that my hesitation was just as much for her sake as it was for mine. "I lost a lot this year, Faye. It would hurt me to lose you too. I don't know how I'd come back from it."

"Trevor," she whispered, "you're not going to lose me. In fact, you're stuck with me…until February."

"Thank God." I chuckled softly, nodding at her. "I want you, sweetheart. I've never wanted any woman on earth as much as I want you." I leaned forward to kiss her. "But my feelings for you are growing really fast, and they're really strong. I'm guessing you feel the same?"

She nodded. "I do."

"Then give yourself a little more time. A few more days. I want you to be sure."

Tilting her head to the side, she stared at me for a long moment, then took a deep breath and let it go. "Okay."

I kissed her again, then headed into the kitchen to pour us each a special New Year's Eve cocktai—

"Trevor? Trev! I've called your name five times, man!"

At some point during my daydream, I had turned my chair around to look out the window in my office, at the traffic in the tasting room. Now I turn back around to find

Baz sitting in a guest chair in front of me. Jesus. I didn't even hear him enter my office.

"Hey."

"Hey," he says, his blue eyes merry. "What were *you* thinking about?"

I grin at him. "I met someone."

"I heard," he tells me.

"You *heard*? I only met her last week!"

"Uh-huh. First from Mom and Dad...then from Cez, via Marlena."

"Well, aren't you just the family's busybody?"

"You've had a shitty few months. We're all..." He shrugs. "Happy for you."

"Yeah, well...we'll see what happens."

"Tell me about her," says Baz, who's always been more of a romantic than me.

I lean forward, folding my hands on my desk. "She's from Boston. She owns one the biggest liquor distribution companies in the country."

"Huh. That's a lucky connection."

It occurs to me that Faye hasn't mentioned buying my company over the last few days, and I wonder if she's given up. I'll miss the banter, but the reality is that I really don't want to sell right now. I like it that my brothers and I are in business together, and I don't want someone else to oversee my company. I still enjoy being a business owner too much to turn over the reins to someone else. Even her.

"She actually came up here to check us out."

"North Star? Really? We're famous as far away as

Boston?"

"I don't know about famous," I say, "but her acquisitions guy called me back in November, poking around about a possible sale. So I guess we've been on their radar, yeah."

"What did you say at the time?"

"No."

"Without talking to me and Cez?"

"I'd buy out your forty-nine percent before I'd let you sell to someone else."

"Can you do that?"

I nod. "Check the contract. I have right of first refusal if either of you ever want to sell."

Baz takes this in for a second, then says, "I talked to Cez."

I take a deep breath, leaning back in my chair. "Yeah. And?"

"He said you didn't hang up on him."

"We didn't talk long either."

"It's progress, Trev."

"Don't read too much into it, Baz."

"And Marlena said she saw you at the hospital."

"She did."

"She said you seemed pretty into the girl you brought in."

"That's almost accurate. I'm *very* into her."

"How's her foot?"

"Still broken."

"She's staying at your place? Until she's better?"

I can't help smiling. I feel like a sap, but fuck it, I can't help it. "Yep."

"Damn, bro! You *like* this girl."

"Yeah, I do. I like her a lot."

"I'm glad, Trev. I'm so fucking glad." He pauses for a second, his smiling fading. "What about Cez? You think…maybe, now that you've met someone else—"

"I don't know how to trust him, Baz." I pause for a second. "Something you said to me a few weeks ago has stuck with me, though—that maybe Marlena and I weren't in the healthiest relationship, and I see it now. I do. We weren't a great match. Not perfect, anyway. But, Baz, he could have come to me. He could've said something."

"What could he have said? 'I'm in love with your fiancée'? 'I want to be with her'? 'Get out of the way'?"

"Better than fucking her on the night before my wedding," I say. "What exactly *was* the plan? For Marlena to go through with it and *marry* me?"

"No," says Baz. "They were going to talk to you after the rehearsal dinner. That's why Marlena went to his room— so they could discuss how best to approach you. And then one thing…"

"Led to another."

"I guess."

"But they'd been sleeping together for a while."

Baz inclines his head. "I think so, yes."

"That sucks, Baz."

"I agree. It does."

But he looks so fucking sad, and I feel so fucking

happy, I have to give him some hope.

"Give it time," I tell my little brother. "Maybe…at some point…when enough time's gone by, we'll find our way back to each other."

He immediately brightens. "I hope so. In the meantime, I'd love to meet…"

"Faye."

"Yes. Faye. Hey! Are you going to Mom's Twelfth Night party this weekend?"

Every year, my mother throws a Twelfth Night party twelve days after Christmas. It's an English tradition that she brought across the pond with her and mostly includes the consumption of wassail, which is a strong alcoholic punch, and a potluck of desserts on a large buffet table, as well as the singing Christmas carols. It's become quite a popular tradition with my parents' friends and alleviates a bit of the Christmas-is-over letdown.

"I don't know," I say, "but probably not. Faye's still in a lot pain. Then again, her sister's coming to town, so—"

"Her sister, huh? Is she pretty?"

"Yeah. If Faye's any indication, then she'll be gorgeous. But she's young. Only twenty."

"That's legal." Baz raises his eyebrows. "How about I swing by on Saturday night. If the sister wants to come with me, I'll take her to the party, and either way, I'll get a chance to meet Faye."

"Promise you won't make a move on her?"

"Faye or the sister?" he asks, standing up from his seat and pushing the guest chair back under my desk.

"Faye," I say, adding a little steel to my voice.

"I'm not Cez," he declares, then half-smiles, half-cringes. "Too soon?"

"*Way* too soon," I tell him, but wonder of wonders, I actually find myself smiling as my little brother leaves my office.

***

Faye

Harry arrived in Fairbanks on Thursday night, and yesterday, we built a nest on the couch in the living room and spent the day chilling out and catching up.

She told me all about Vail, and I was proud of her when she told me that she and Austin remain friends.

I told her all about Trevor—excluding the part about answering a personal ad, which, Trevor and I decided, would be our secret. We ended the day with Chinese takeout that Trevor picked up for us at the Golden Buddha, and Harry fell asleep with her head on my shoulder as we watched a Christmas movie on the Hallmark Channel.

Today, Saturday, we've spent some time driving around Fairbanks, sightseeing with Trevor—we showed her the distillery and tasting room, in addition to visiting a reindeer farm, where Harry could meet and pet some reindeer and take a short hike with them.

Her cheeks are bright red from the cold, but she's beaming from ear to ear when she returns to the car.

"Faye! When you're feeling better, we have to go back! They had little baby reindeer! So darling!"

I've never enjoyed Harry quite as much I have during

this visit.

It's like I've finally given myself permission to get to know her, to love her not just as a sibling or dependent but as an adult and friend. No credit to me, but she's such a smart, positive, fun-loving person—I think anybody who meets her must fall a little bit in love with her. And with thick, chestnut-colored hair she wears long and straight; wide, kind brown eyes; and a trim size-six figure, it's no wonder Harry's had her share of conquests: she's beautiful.

"What's next?" she asks, buckling herself into the back seat.

"How do you feel about going to a party tonight?" asks Trevor as he pulls out of the reindeer farm parking lot.

"Awesome! I love parties!"

I shift in my seat a little to face her in the back seat. "Trevor's brother, Baz, is coming over for preparty drinks. He can take you if you want to go."

Her smile dims a touch. "Wait. Aren't you two going?"

"I'm sorry, Harry," I say gently. "But I've been up on this foot more yesterday and today than I've been since I broke it. I need to relax tonight."

Honestly, I am tired, but I *may* have been up for the party if I could have sat on the couch at Trevor's parent's house once I was there. The thing is, Trevor specifically said he didn't want to go. He's still not ready to see Cecil, and while I hope he finds space in his heart to forgive his brother at some point, I also understand that he needs more time.

"Gotcha," says Harry with a sigh. "But I'm not here for very long. Maybe I should stay home with you, Faye."

"You don't have to," I tell her. "I'll probably just go to bed early."

This is partially true. Also true? With Harry in town and staying in the guest room across the hall from us, Trevor and I haven't had much privacy. I'm sort of longing to have some alone time with him tonight. So yes. I may go to bed early, but he'll be coming with me.

"Are you sure? I mean…I hate to leave you, but I *love* a party."

"Absolutely positive," I tell her. "Baz can take you to Starling Farms for the festivities and bring you home whenever you're ready, right?"

I look at Trevor, who knows exactly what I'm doing. He winks at me with twinkling eyes before speaking up: "Right. Exactly. And take your time, Harry. No need to rush home. My mother makes a killer wassail."

***

While Harry's upstairs getting ready for the annual Starling Twelfth Night party, Trevor and I sit side by side on the couch in front of the fireplace, my head on his shoulder and our hands laced together. There's an excellent bottle of merlot in front of us with two half-drunk glasses resting on the coffee table.

I'm tired after driving all over Fairbanks today, as evidenced by a loud yawn that takes me by surprise.

"Sorry!" I say.

Trevor chuckles beside me. "I guess you weren't kidding about going to bed early, huh, sweetheart?"

I grin at him, feeling warm and sleepy. "I guess I

wasn't."

"I'll carry you upstairs as soon as Harry's off."

"Or maybe…"

"Maybe what?" he asks.

"You said you have a hot tub downstairs, right?"

"Mm-hm. You want to go tubbing?"

"It would be so nice to dunk these weary muscles in hot water," I say. "Would it be too much trouble?"

"Umm. To have my girlfriend all to myself in a hot tub? No. Not trouble. I'll turn it on when Baz gets here so it's nice and warm for us."

I gasp when he says this for one simple reason: I have never been anyone's girlfriend before this moment, and it's so sweet and so fun to hear him say the words, it takes my breath away.

"What?" he asks, scanning my face. "What happened?"

"You called me your girlfriend," I say softly, blinking at him.

He grins. "Oh. Yeah. I did. Is that okay?"

I start nodding, and then my eyes fill with tears—*when did I become so emotional?*—and I'm giggling and nodding and trying not to cry when he cups my face and touches his lips to mine. He kisses me thoroughly, passionately, his tongue slipping between my lips to find mine in an action so familiar to me now, I savor the taste and texture of him, while the rest of my body aches for the same kind of intimacy. He wants me to wait a few more days until we have sex, but I'm frustrated with the waiting. If I am not already in love with him, I am surely on the verge. And though I don't know what the future holds, each day I spend with Trevor makes me long for my future to be entwined irrevocably with his. That's all I know. But it's enough—more than enough—for me to know I want to give myself to him physically. I have no reservations left. None. It's just a matter of finding the right time now.

"Oh, my God, you guys! Get a room!"

I yank back from Trevor to face my sister, and I immediately feel my cheeks go up in flames. I've never been caught "making out" with someone before, and to be caught by my little sister feels beyond embarrassing.

"Faye!" she exclaims, sitting on the back of the couch. "I'm just kidding. Oh, my God, lighten up."

She chucks Trevor lightly on the cheek. "Be nice to my sister, now."

"Don't worry, Little Bit," he says. "I like her way too much to be mean."

He's been calling Harry "Little Bit" all weekend, and I know she likes it because she wrinkles her nose and grins whenever he says it.

The doorbell rings from downstairs, and Trevor sits up.

"Ah! That's Baz." He kisses my nose. "I'll be right back!"

He slides off the couch, leaving me and Harry alone. She circles the couch, standing between the coffee table and the mantle. She gestures to the wineglasses. "Which is yours?"

"The one on the left."

She picks it up and takes a sip, and I stare at her—at my

beautiful sister, dressed in jeans, a white turtleneck, and a Cornell sweat shirt—backlit by the fire.

I will always have my regrets—about not being there for her, about not showing her how much I have loved her all these years, about not sharing our lives the way sisters can and should for so long—but right this minute, I'm so grateful for our new beginning, all I feel is…love. Heaping, brimming spoonfuls of love.

"I love you, Harry," I say.

She tilts her head to the side. "I love you too."

"Have we ever said that to each other?" I ask. "In person?"

"No."

I swallow over the lump in my throat. "I'm sorry."

"Don't be," she says, taking another sip of wine before putting the glass back on the table. "You were a kid when they died. Only two years older than I am now. I can't imagine finishing my MBA, taking over the company, dealing with Mama and Daddy's estate, and becoming the guardian of a little sister." She sniffles softly. "You did great, Faye."

"I did…okay," I say. "Not great. From now on, I'm going to do great."

She leans down and kisses my cheek. "You already are."

We hear footsteps coming up from the lower level of the house, and both of us look toward the kitchen landing, where Trevor and a slightly younger, slightly shorter version of Trevor appear. Baz. The family resemblance is uncanny.

"Merlot good for you?" Trevor asks his brother, stopping in the kitchen for two more wineglasses.

"Uh…y-yeah. Great. What…ever."

Baz—who has bright-blue eyes, the same thick dark hair as Trevor, and a close-cropped black beard—is standing beside the dining table, utterly undone, looking over my head with struck-dumb enchantment at…Harry. I turn my neck slowly to glance up at my sister, whose lips are parted with a similar small smile. Two soft-pink spots appear on her cheeks, and she bites down on her bottom lip for a second before letting it go.

"Hi," she says, giving a little wave. "I'm Harry—um, Harriet…Findley."

"Basil Starling," he answers, still staring at her as though in a trance.

I catch Trevor's face over his brother's shoulder, and he raises an eyebrow. *What's going on here?*

I give him a little shrug. *I have no idea.*

"Um," says Trevor, putting an arm around his brother's shoulder and leading him over to the sitting area. "Baz, this is my girlfriend, Faye. Faye, this is my brother Baz."

For the first time, Baz seems to notice me sitting on the couch, lowers his gaze, and offers me his hand.

"Hey…Hey, Faye." He clears his throat, flicking a glance back up at Harry before focusing on me. "Trev is…crazy about you. I'm glad to, you know, meet you."

"Thanks," I say, grinning at him. "I'm crazy about your brother too."

"That's good. That's…really good," says Baz, looking up at Harry again. He slides his hand away from me and offers it to my sister. "I'm Baz."

I watch Harry's eyes sparkle and shine as she takes Baz's hand in hers. "Harry."

"You're...*stunning*, Harry."

She smiles at him, biting that lower lip again. *Oh, Harry...you* like *him.* "Thank you."

Trevor picks up the bottle of merlot and pours each of them a glass of wine, then hands me mine.

"To the new year," he says, staring into my eyes as he makes the toast. "In it, may all of our dreams come true!"

"Here, here," says Harry, grinning at Baz as she tilts her glass back and sips.

Trevor resumes his seat next to me, while Harry takes the chair to my right and Baz takes a seat across from her, to Trevor's left.

"So, Harry," says Baz, "how long are you visiting?"

"Only until Monday," she says. "I leave for Seattle early on Monday morning."

"I see," he says, his brows creasing a lot like his brother's as he nods. He looks at me. "But you'll be around for a while longer, Faye?"

"Yes," I say, gesturing to the boot. "Until mid-February."

"At least," mumbles Trevor.

I look over at him, wondering what he means.

"Did you tell Harry about the party?" asks Baz.

"We did," says Trevor, glancing at my sister. "What did you decide, Little Bit?"

"I thought I'd go," she says, turning to me, "if you're sure you're okay without me?"

I grin at her. "We'll manage somehow."

"Best not drink anymore for now, then, if I'm driving you." Baz places his glass down on the table. "So…want to get going?"

Harry giggles. "Sure."

I look back and forth between them and smile, because I don't know what I'm witnessing here, but it certainly feels like the beginning of *something*.

Harry leans down to kiss me on the cheek and whispers, "Don't wait up," all saucy, winking at me before she grabs her jacket and purse off a dining room chair. I watch with approval as Baz gently takes the jacket from her and holds it open so she can slip into it.

"Have fun, you two!" calls Trevor from the couch.

"Thanks!" they call from the stairs leading down to the basement.

Once I hear the lower level door slam shut, I turn to Trevor. "Are you playing matchmaker?"

"Who? Me?"

"So innocent," I say, giving him a look. "Be honest."

"Honestly," he says, "no. Though if I was, your sister couldn't be in safer hands. Baz moves at the speed of…molasses. In Alaska. In January." He stands up. "Ready to go hot-tubbing?"

"Yes," I tell him, looping my arms around his neck as he lifts me. "Just for clarification…what does that mean? To move at the speed of molasses?"

He adjusts me in his arms, and I lay my head against his shoulder as he walks toward the stairs to the lower level.

"Hmm. Well, before tonight, mind you, because I think we just watched my brother fall head over heels for your sister, he had a crush on our marketing advisor, Penny. Except we've been working with Penny for over three years, and Baz has yet to ask her out."

"Ah. Okay. So you're being literal."

"Uh-huh," he says, getting to the bottom of the stairs and turning right toward the TV and game room. "He dated this girl in high school, Elena, who he was crazy about. Everyone thought they'd end up married."

"What happened?"

"She went to college in Anchorage, met someone new, got married down there, and hasn't really been back since."

"Oh God."

"Yeah. I mean, Baz is twenty-five, and I still don't think he's over it."

"She was his one and only?" I ask as he sets me down carefully on a chair beside the hot tub and starts taking off the cover to reveal tendrils of steam rising from the roiling water.

"She was. And I mean, I've noticed he lights up when Penny's around, so I thought he might ask her out sometime, but Baz is quiet, you know? Thoughtful. Introspective. He's strong, but he's a lover, not a fighter."

I reach down and unbuckle my boot.

Trevor looks over at me. "Do you want the door open?"

He's referring to a garage door that can open to let in the cold air and offer an unrestricted view of the mountains behind his house. "Whatever you prefer."

While he opens the door, I take off my shirt and sweat shirt, so I'm only wearing my pajama shorts and a bra. When I look up, Trevor's staring at me, looking as dumbfounded as his brother earlier. His eyes drop to my breasts, and without thinking twice, I reach behind my back, unlatch my bra, and let it skim down my arms.

His lips part. His eyes widen. His nostrils flare.

"Do you—um—have a bathing suit or—"

"Nope."

"Do you want me to, um…hmm…um…" He gulps, standing a few feet away from me, this strong, savvy, experienced businessman reduced to a sputtering caveman because my breasts are naked.

How empowering, I think, grinning to myself and maybe arching my back a little so that my breasts stick out more.

"I could use some help getting my shorts off," I tell him, trying out a lower and softer voice than usual.

He blinks at me, licking his lips. "Um. Yeah. So…we're skinny-dipping? That's cool. That's a…good idea."

"Boot first," I say, as he stands before me.

He kneels down, takes it gently between his hands, and pulls it off, leaning it against the chair. When he looks up at me, his eyes are so full of adoration, it would humble me if I wasn't feeling so full of myself.

I stand up, bearing my weight on my good foot and letting the broken one dangle. Never breaking contact with his eyes, I slip my fingers into the waistband of my shorts.

"You do it." I order him. "Pull them down."

He takes over for my fingers, and slowly, so slowly, he slides my shorts and panties down my thighs and knees, letting them fall to my ankle in a whisper. When I'm naked before him, he stares up at me, his green eyes dark and liquid, so full of emotion, it makes my heart clench, then soar.

"I'm falling in love with you," he tells me.

"I am too," I say. "Falling in love with you."

Then he stands up, swoops me into his arms, and deposits me gently into the hot tub.

CHAPTER TWELVE

Faye

Once I'm settled in the hot water, sitting on a bench built into the side of the tub, Trevor steps away, turning his back to me.

"Trevor."

He looks over his shoulder at me as he's about to take off his long-sleeved T-shirt. "Huh?"

"Turn around."

His lips tilt up and eyes widen. "You want to watch?"

I nod. "It's only fair."

"Sweetheart," he says, turning around completely. "I live to be fair."

I raise my arms like Hugh Hefner, spreading them out along the rim of the tub, my nipples peeking above the surface of the moving water.

"Proceed, sir."

Slowly, moving his hips a little and—if I'm not mistaken—flexing his chest, he lifts his T-shirt over his head and throws it on the ground. I sigh softly, looking at the muscles on his chest that have been lifting me and carrying me for almost a week now. I've felt them behind me as we sleep, and even slept with my hands flattened against his chest, but I've never seen him on display like this before now.

"Well," I murmur. "That's…lovely."

He raises his eyebrows at me and grins. "Ready for more?"

"Uh-huh."

"I have to warn you, I'm going commando today."

I feel my face screw up in confusion. "You're a commando? Like…in the military?"

He chuckles softly. "It means I'm not wearing underwear."

"What?" I know my eyes are bugging out of my head. "None?"

"Not a thread."

"Isn't that…uncomfortable?"

"Not when I'm wearing sweats around the house."

"Well, then," I say, ignoring my blush and gesturing with my hand, like a queen to a courtier, "get on with it."

He laughs again, slipping his fingers into the waistband of his gray sweat pants and tugging them over his hips. To maneuver them over his erect penis, he has to pull them out and over, then lets them drop to the floor.

And there he is: Trevor Starling, my boyfriend, my man, the first and only love of my life, standing like Adonis, gloriously naked before me.

"Any other instructions?" he asks.

"Mm-hm," I hum. "Come here. I'm lonely."

He laughs again, and I this time, I laugh with him because playing the coquette for the first time in my life is stupid amounts of fun.

I watch as he climbs into the tub with me, sitting across from me on the bench.

"Why so far away?" I pout.

"Who *are* you?" he asks.

"Faye Findley."

"Actually," he says, "tonight, I think you're Faith Crawford."

"Fine," I tell him, reaching out my arms. "I'm Faith Crawford too."

He takes my hands and lets me pull him across the tub, squatting in front of me so that his shoulders are above water, but the rest of him is below.

"I'd hold you on my lap, but I'm hard as a rock, sweetheart."

It takes me a second to understand he's talking about his erection, but once I do, I reach out for it under the water. "Yes. You are."

"Ahhhh." His eyes close, and his hands land on the rim of the tub behind me, bracketing me between his outstretched arms.

I don't know a lot about giving a man pleasure, but I know that when he rubs my clitoris, it feels amazing, so using that same logic, I rub him up and down, varying the speed and pressure of my grip until he's panting faster and faster.

"Faye, I'm going to...I'm going to..." He releases a strangled cry, and his body tenses like crazy for a second before he relaxes, his head rolling back as he takes a deep breath and sighs with satisfaction.

The motion of the hot tub sweeps away any evidence of his climax, as he sits down next to me, giving me a dazed, contented grin. "That's been building up for a while."

"Oh! Oh no! I'm sorry."

It should have occurred to me that he was suffering. He did, after all, place the ad to meet a woman for sex.

"Faye," he says, reaching for my face and making me look at him. "I'd wait a million years for you. Don't be sorry."

"But the ad…you wanted…"

"That ad," he scoffs. "I had no idea what I really wanted. I was lonely, and I thought having sex would help, but I was a fool."

"Having sex won't help?"

He smiles at me, caressing my cheek with the back of his hand before leaning forward to kiss me tenderly. "Having sex will be amazing. With you. When you're ready."

And at that moment? That crazy sexy moment?

I yawn.

I freaking *yawn*.

"I'm…oh no. I'm not tired."

He smiles at me. "Yes, sweetheart, you are. You're exhausted. How about I carry you up to bed, and we resume this another time?"

"No," I insist. "I'm good. I'm—"

And fuck me, but I yawn! Again.

"Time for bed," says Trevor, standing up and stepping out of the tub. There's a neat stack of towels sitting on a teak stool, and he takes one, wrapping it around his waist. "Can you stand up?"

Reluctantly, and feeling a little disappointed in my lack of physical stamina, I stand on my good leg and let Trevor lift me out of the tub. He places my naked body on the chair where I got undressed and turns around to grab another towel.

"Up again," he commands gently. "Arms up."

He wraps me up like a burrito, then dips his head to kiss me. "I swear to God, Faye, I don't mind the wait."

"But I do," I tell him, openly pouting. "I want you, T. I'm ready."

"You're exhausted," he whispers, still holding my face between his hands. He nuzzles my nose with his. "We have plenty of time."

I let him sweep me into his arms, and by the time we reach his bedroom, I'm nodding off. He places me on my side of the bed, covering me with his soft flannel sheets and warm duvet.

"Go to sleep. I'll bring up your boot in a bit and get it back on your foot."

"Thank you," I murmur, nestling into the pillow, "my love."

"You're welcome," he says, kissing my forehead as I quickly fall asleep.

***

When I wake up the next morning, the first thing I realize is that I'm naked under the covers.

The towel from last night came undone and is now

flattened beneath me.

I also realize, from the heat radiating into my hip, that Trevor is naked too, but his towel is bunched between our legs. I shove at it with my good foot until it's not between us anymore, then peek at my boyfriend, who's lying on his back and still fast asleep.

Sliding my phone from the bedside table, I check for messages and find one from Harry.

> HARRIET: We drank 2 much wassail. Barb insisted we stay overnight. Baz & I are in T's old room. I'm on the top bunk & he's on the bottom. It was such a fun party! I'm going to stay for brunch tomorrow, so I'll see you sometime in the afternoon. Love u!

I put my phone back on the table and maneuver myself onto the office chair that Trevor kindly left beside the bed. After I take a moment to pee, wash my face, and brush my teeth, I roll back to bed, stark naked, to find Trevor's eyes open. He's on his side, leaning up on one elbow, wearing nothing but a grin.

"Good morning," he says.

For no good reason—or maybe, it occurs to me, with a suddenly and growing anticipation, for a *very* good reason—I feel a little shy. "Hi."

Trevor pats my empty spot on the bed. "Come back."

"We're naked."

He nods. "Yes, we are."

"This is it, isn't it?" I say. "We're going to…"

"If you want to," he says, his beautiful eyes soft and sexy.

229

"I do," I say. But I don't move. "Is it okay that I'm a little scared?"

"Faye, if you're not ready—"

"I *am* ready," I tell him, backing the chair up to the bed, pushing off from the ground with my good foot, and transferring my body onto the mattress. I look at him over my bare shoulder. "I'm ready...and I want you...in every way...but I can still be a little scared, Trevor."

He leans up, reaching under my arms to pull me back, closer to him. I twist at the waist and lie down on my back, turning my head to look at him. He reaches for my face with his hand, cupping my cheek, and I roll to my side, facing him.

"You don't need to be scared."

But even with several inches of space between us, I can feel the tip of his erect penis pressing into my stomach. It's long, hard and hot against my skin, and it makes me tingle with want, even as I hold my breath, wondering how my much smaller body will accommodate the girth and length of his.

"It might hurt," I whisper.

He tries not to smile.

"For a moment, and then never again," he says.

"Promise?"

"I promise, sweetheart."

I want this. I want him. So much.

I take a deep breath and nod. "Kiss me."

Laying his hand on my waist, he pulls me closer, so that the front of my body is flush with the front of his. My breasts are crushed against his pecs, and the points of my nipples are tickled by the hair on his chest. The base of his erection presses hot and insistent against the folds that cover my pulsating clit, while his length strains against the soft skin of my belly.

"Okay?" he asks, looking into my eyes, his smile reassuring.

"Mm-hm," I hum, nodding at him. I'm nervous. I'm also trusting him with every fiber of my being. "Okay."

Once he's given me a second or two to get used to our naked bodies touching so intimately, he leans forward and touches his lips to mine. Gently. Tentatively. But it's all I need to feel back in control of what's happening between us, because I *know* this. Kissing him is familiar to me now. I reach for him, rolling onto my back and encouraging him to come with me. He slides his tongue between my lips, careful not to hit my boot with his legs as he settles on top of me. Stealing my breath as he deepens our kiss, I can feel my body tuning up, like an orchestra about to play a concerto.

He kisses my neck, taking my earlobe between his teeth and biting it gently as I squeal with delight, then demand his lips back again. All the while, his erection presses against me, hot and hard, before slipping into the slick channel that hides my clit. When the ridges of muscle massage my rigid bud of nerves, I moan into Trevor's mouth.

"Oh, my God..."

He leans up to look into my eyes, which are half-masted with pleasure.

"Good?" he asks me, his voice raspy with emotion.

"*So* good," I tell him, pulling him back down to kiss me while his hips continue to surge forward, rubbing against me until I'm whimpering and moaning, my breath coming in shallow pants as he moves faster and faster, bracing his body by planting his hands on either side of my head, his pelvis surging forward then pulling back, my clit on the verge of explosion.

"Trevor...Trev ...T..." I pant, feeling myself coming apart, about to come.

"I want to be inside of you," he says, his voice straining and rough.

"Yes," I say. "I want that...too..."

He pauses. "You're sure?"

"I'm...on the pill," I tell him.

"I know," he tells me, because Mr. Fairbanks insisted.

My clit still hums and vibrates, but it's greedy too—I want satisfaction. I want to feel him—all of him—inside of me. And I want us to orgasm together.

"I'm ready," I tell him. "I want this, I want you."

He reaches down, positioning the tip of his erection at the opening of my sex.

"Don't tense," he says, leaning down to kiss me tenderly. "It'll be better if you don't."

I take a deep breath, hyperaware of my body as he slowly moves forward. It's so strange and surreal, after so long, to be having sex for the first time in my life, but at the same time, I absorb every movement, every panted breath, every hesitation and advance. We are in this together, and I have never felt more cherished in my entire life.

He winces, and I realize that he's likely come upon my virgin barrier.

"It'll only hurt for a second," he says.

I nod. "Then never again."

"Then never, ever again," he promises, leaning down to kiss me, distracting me as he thrusts forward, making me totally and completely his.

Do I feel a pinch as he pushes through? I do.

Does it pass quickly? Thank the gods of sex, it does.

For a few seconds, he is completely still, and how he manages that after not having had sex in months, I don't know. But he leans up from our kiss and looks down at my face, holding himself frozen.

"Are you," he pants, a sheen of sweat beading on his forehead, "okay?"

"Yeah," I murmur, my voice breathless but also a little excited. I did it. We did it! The deed is done! The weight of my virginity rolls off my shoulders, and I wiggle my hips a little, wanting to learn more, try everything I've only read or dreamt about. "I am."

At some point, I had fisted the sheet by my hips in a tight grip, but now I unfurl my fingers, skimming them over the smooth, warm planes of his back, loving the feeling of his body on top of mine, embedded within mine.

"Sure?" he asks, grinning at me with wonder.

"Yeah. It doesn't hurt," I say. "It's…good." I giggle softly. "I want more, T."

He leans down to brush his lips against my cheek, his nose nuzzling mine, as he pulls his hips back, then lets them surge forward again.

This time, I feel the full measure of his length, the way his sex fill me, and how my inner walls grasp onto him. I flex my muscles, and he groans.

"You like that?" I ask, reveling in this new information.

"I...like that...sweetheart," he half-murmurs, half-grunts, his eyes closed. I do it again—tighten, then release—watching him grimace with pleasure, before opening his eyes. "Faye...it's been a long time...for me."

His voice is strangled, and I realize that while I'm experimenting with him, he's just holding on.

"Let go, my love," I tell him, reaching up to place my hands on his cheeks and drawing his lips down to mine. "Make love to me."

Kissing me with abandon, he thrusts into me in a more steady rhythm, slowly at first, then faster and faster, and I thank God for the preparation of kissing and touching before penetration, because I am wet and slick, taking his surges forward with pleasure, not pain.

He reaches for my good leg, pulling it up so that I am opened wider to him, and with his other hand he holds my head, still kissing me, his tongue swirling around mine before he pants into my neck, his breath coming in short bursts as his thrusts become rhythmic and fast. His hips buck forward again and again, and I am lost in a vortex of his movements. I exist for his pleasure...and for mine, which builds and builds within me.

Releasing my thigh, he wedges his hand between our bodies, his finger sliding with precision to land on my glistening clit, which he circles and strokes. I thrash my head back into the pillow, arching my back, my hips bucking off the bed as I orgasm.

Not a moment later, his forehead falls against my neck as he cries out my name, his body freezing, then trembling and shaking over mine. I feel his release deep within me, the hot spurts of his seed inside of me, and I welcome them, holding him close as he pants by my ear, and shudders with aftershocks.

Sighing deeply, he rocks gently into me. Slowly. Softly. Tenderly.

When I feel wetness on my cheeks, I realize with some surprise that I'm crying, and when I take a deep breath, it's ragged and uneven. I don't know what's brought on tears, but I can only imagine it's because in my entire adult life, I've never felt as precious to another human being as I do to Trevor right this minute, and it's…overwhelming. In a good way. But still.

He leans up to look at me, his eyes dilated, his skin slick with sweat. "Oh…no. You're crying. What is it? Are you okay?"

I sniffle, winding my arms around his neck when he tries to pull away from me. I want him to stay where he is, connected to me in a deeply intimate, incredibly beautiful way. I want to stay like this forever.

"I…" I pause because the words on the tip of my tongue are "I love you," but I'm not sure I'm ready to say them yet. Instead, I nod, mustering a small smile and say, "Thank you, Trevor. For being so gentle. So caring. That was…*so beautiful.*"

"My sweetheart," he murmurs, leaning up on his elbows, and grinning down at me as he cups my face, "that's only the beginning."

***

Trevor

When you're happy—when you are really and truly, blissfully happy, like you've never been before in your entire life—time moves so fast, it makes your head spin. It makes you regret all the days you ever spent wasting it.

Two weeks later, Faye and I have settled into a routine with each other, diligently working at our respective companies during the day, but the nights…*God,* the nights.

At the wedding of my mother's younger brother to my Scottish aunt, they exchanged vows that included the words "With my body, I thee worship," and at the time, my teenage heart was secretly fascinated by these words. It was a romantic sentiment, for sure, but it was also an incredibly sexy image to invoke in the middle of a church service.

It's always stuck with me—that idea of worshipping someone's body…though, despite many lovers during my life, I've never actually *experienced* the feeling invoked in those vows…until now.

I worship Faye's body every night.

I touch and taste, explore and learn, pleasure and adore. Unreservedly.

And she gives herself to me with a trust and generosity that humbles me and that I will never betray while there's breath in my body.

We talk for hours on end, and I feel understood in ways I've only ever dreamt of being known. She *gets* me—all of me, and I get her too. We are driven and focused but can be distracted with playfulness or teasing. We try different wines at night with the dinners Inez makes for us, and I think I've introduced Faye to a few vodka infusions she's never tried before. She tells me about her life in the "before" when her parents were still alive, and the "after," when she was left alone with Findley Imports and a little sister to raise on her own. I tell her about growing up with hippie parents and twin brothers, in a family where rowdiness and mindfulness were encouraged. She laughs when I refuse to talk about selling my company, and I laugh when she insists it'll be hers someday. One day, when I'm deep inside of her and she's sighing my name, I might say yes because she feels so good, so right, that I'd agree to just about anything...but luckily, we haven't mixed business and sex...yet.

My life is so good, so full, that I have begun to think a lot about the future. And specifically, how Faye fits into that future, because, more and more, the only life I can see for myself anymore is one that includes Faye Findley.

A month from now, give or take, Faye will be given the "okay" to fly again. And once that happens, she could leave—probably *will* leave unless we have a plan for her to stay—which is a thought that constricts my throat and feels unbearable to the extreme.

Call it fast.

Call it insta-love.

I don't care.

It happens sometimes.

It's happened to me.

I know what I know: that I am falling deeply in love with her in a way I've never known before. I want her *in* my life for the *rest* of my life, not just for the time she's trapped here. And not with distance separating us either. I'm not sure I could bear a relationship that goes from daily intimacy to phone calls and text chats, to hurried couplings in airport hotels once a month when we carve out some time.

I want us together every day and every night.

I'm pretty sure what I want with Faye Findley is…forever.

I'm just not sure that forever with me is what she wants too, because we haven't discussed it yet. That said, I have made a study of the recent changes in Faye's life and how's she's handled them…and her behavior gives me hope.

Since we speak freely and with enthusiasm about our businesses, I know that Faye has had to delegate a great deal of her responsibilities to Karl Franklin, her former VP of acquisitions, whom she promoted to interim-CEO of Findley Imports.

I also know that the meeting Karl and Harry took with UNNW in Seattle was a success, and UNNW is selling to Findley Imports in a private transaction on March 1, pending legal due diligence and the signing of contracts.

The net-net of these two developments in Faye's company could be good for us on a personal level, I think.

Opening an office in Seattle means that Faye, as president of Findley Imports, can work from Boston *or*

Seattle. And Alaska Airlines flights from Fairbanks to Seattle are arranged so that folks can commute. Flights leave Fairbanks early in the morning, you can spend a full workday in Seattle, and easily be home in time for bed. Not that I'd want Faye to have to make that trip more than once or twice a week, because it's a three-and-a-half-hour commute each way, but staying together would, in fact, be...*possible*, especially with her new delegation skills. She isn't counting on herself to be the sole leader of Findley Imports anymore. Breaking her foot has forced her to choose those employees she trusts to take on more responsibility, allowing her more time to recover *now*...and for her personal life *later*.

Leaning against my kitchen counter as the Keurig spits out a cup of coffee on a cold Sunday morning, I consider asking her to move in with me, but for all that we live in the twenty-first century, I still consider myself old-fashioned about some things, and asking Faye to uproot her life in Boston and move to Alaska should come with a bigger commitment from me than having a key made.

Like maybe...having a *ring* made.

Yes, that's where my mind is right now.

Not even a year after my ex-fiancée slept with my brother the night before our wedding, I'm thinking about getting married again.

But I can honestly say, with one hundred percent certainty, that Marlena was not destiny. Faye is my destiny. I know this in my marrow, like it was embedded into my DNA at the beginning of my days. I am meant to be with Faye Findley, and she is meant to be with me.

I step out of the kitchen and pause at the bottom of the stairs.

"Sweetheart! You want coffee?"

"Yes! Thanks!" she yells from her office.

I place a second cup under the Keurig spout while I add a touch of almond milk and dash of Stevia to hers. I prefer mine black, but I know exactly how Faye likes hers.

Heading back upstairs with our mugs, I pause in the doorway of the guest room to check her out from behind. She's leaning over her desk, typing out what appears to be an email.

"Anything interesting?" I ask.

She looks at me over her shoulder. "Maybe."

"Want to tell me about it?" I ask, handing her the coffee, then backing up to the doorway and leaning against it. I don't want to interrupt her if she's in the middle of work.

"I think I like Karl in the position of CEO," she says. "And me as president of the company and chairman of the board."

"Okay."

"Which means…" she says, taking a sip of her coffee and spinning around in her chair to face me. "Ooh. It's perfect."

I chuckle because she's adorable and I love her.

I *love* her.

Whoa.

I love her.

I think I knew, I just hadn't…told myself yet.

But it feels right. In fact, it feels perfect. *I love her.*

"What?" she asks, no doubt seeing my face process the words spoken by my heart.

Part of me is dying to tell her, but I'm not just going to blurt it out. There will be a better time. A better moment.

"Umm. What were you saying? You said, 'Which means…'"

"Oh! Yes. Which means I need to find a CEO to run the Seattle operations too."

"And then you'll…"

"Well, I'll still be ultimately in charge of both offices, Seattle and Boston, but I didn't realize how much delegating could free me up to think more globally for my business, you know? I'm enjoying that freedom."

"I think it's a great decision," I tell her—and has the added benefit of not requiring her to work full time at either office.

"You think?"

I nod. "I do. Especially because…"

She tilts her head to the side. "What?"

"It would make it easier for you to stay."

"In Fairbanks?" She stares at me. "But I have a house in Boston."

"I know."

"And my company's headquartered in Boston."

"I know that too," I say, reaching up to rub the back of my neck. I raise my mug to my lips and sip. This isn't going the way I'd imagined it in my daydreams. "I'm not being clear. What I'm really saying, Faye, is that I want us to figure out a way to stay together."

Her face. Oh, my heart, her sweet face softens with tenderness, and she gasps softly. "You want to stay together? With me? After February?"

"I want to stay together…with you…" I place my coffee on the bureau to my right, then cross the room, falling to my knees in front of her. "Indefinitely."

"Me too. I want that too, Trevor," she says, reaching for my face. She holds it tenderly, staring into my eyes. "But I don't know how it looks yet."

Neither do I, if she won't commute from Fairbanks to Seattle, because I don't want to live in Boston. But I figure we have time and space to figure all that out. For now, I just want to enjoy the fact that we want to stay together, that we want to make our relationship work.

In related news, know what's awesome about your girlfriend working out of your spare bedroom? There's a bed right behind you.

I lift her from her chair and place her on the bed, untying her bathrobe and spreading it open. Underneath, she wears panties and nothing else.

Suddenly hungry to taste her, I pull her panties down and kneel between her legs. Parting the lips that hide her clit, I lean down and lick a circle around the little bud, kissing gently. Holding her hips firmly, I can feel her moving closer to me. I suck on her clit, then lick it quickly, flicking my tongue back and forth over her nerves until she whimpers, then I back off a little. I don't want her to come yet. I want her soaked and slick when I enter her. I want us to come together.

I reach under her thighs, drawing her closer to my face and sucking harder. I'm listening to her moans, to the way her whimpers are coming faster and faster. When her hips buck off the bed, I lean up, yank down my boxers, and slide inside of her.

She cries out, orgasming for the first time as my cock fills her. Hot and slippery, she takes my full length, curling her fingernails into my ass as I withdraw, then push forward again. Meeting me thrust for thrust, the friction of our movements has me coming fast, and just as she orgasms again, the tremors of her body rocking me from the inside, I feel my own release, which makes me groan and strain. I contract and relax, contract and relax, unconscious motions that result in waves of bliss, and fill her womb with my seed.

My lips brush her neck, then rest over her racing pulse.

Now *is the moment*, I think. *I need her to know.*

"I love you, Faye," I whisper near her ear, my voice still breathless from making love. "I know it's quick, but don't doubt it. It's true, sweetheart. I am *completely* in love with you."

She gasps softly but doesn't say anything.

I don't move, still intimately connected to her, still covering her naked body with mine.

Seconds tick by, feeling like hours, and finally, when I can't stand the silence anymore, when a small part of me begins to fear that perhaps she can't or doesn't return my feelings, I lift my head and look into her glistening eyes...which tell me everything I need to know before she even utters a word.

Gently, I touch my lips to hers, loving her, reassuring her, sealing my feelings with a tender kiss.

"I d-don't d-doubt it," she sobs, as tears stream down her face. She takes a deep breath, and lets it go slowly, holding my eyes with hers. "I know it's true, Trevor. I know...because I love you too."

CHAPTER THIRTEEN

Valentine's Day

Faye

The printed note on my pillow reads,

A FAIRBANKS AFFAIR
Tall, dark, and *very* taken distiller owner
requires the company of the Boston-born
businesswoman who has stolen his heart,
for an intimate Valentine's celebration.
Two of us. One bed.
Zero clothes.

A car's coming at 7:00 p.m.
Pack an overnight bag.
I love you.
T

I read the note again and again, marveling that only two months ago, I was sitting in Dr. Lafferty's office, about to get a cavity filled, when I happened upon Trevor's ad. I thought I'd go to Fairbanks, lose my virginity to a tall dark stranger, and be back in Boston by the second of the year.

Little did I know how much that ad would change my life.

Since deciding that we wanted to stay together, I've really had to think about what I want out of life.

I've reflected a great deal on how losing my parents took away my liberty, took away my freedom of choice, took away any chance of personal election over my own future. Whatever "open road" I thought I had as a twenty-one-year-old was ripped away from me.

Suddenly, I owned a company, which meant I was responsible for the livelihoods of hundreds of employees. At an age where I should have been meeting young men and dating, I was thrust into the role of parenting my sister. And for the ensuing decade, between running Findley Imports and caring for Harry, I had very little time for myself.

I don't know who I would have been if a terrible freak accident hadn't made all my life choices for me, if I'd been able to make them on my own. But I do know that I will not allow the rest of my life to be controlled or guided by circumstances beyond my control.

I'm in control, and this is what I know:

I love Trevor. And I love my sister.

They are the two most important people in my life, but if I am to have a life that includes them in any lasting and meaningful way—that allows for leisurely sex and a delicious brunch every Sunday morning with my boyfriend...or camping out on a couch with my sister and a bottle of wine until she falls asleep on my shoulder—I am going to have to take back the reins and make some serious decisions about my future.

For starters, I can't live full time in Boston anymore.

It's too far from Trevor, who has his business and family in Fairbanks, and Harry, who has applied to West Coast schools for her MBA. I've decided that the most logical course of action would be to sell my house in Newton and maintain small apartments in Boston and Seattle, for when I need to be in either city for business.

Speaking of my little sister, who talks to Baz Starling almost as frequently as she talks to me, Harry has decided to spend spring break in Fairbanks. Her *actual* words were "I want to come home for spring break, Faye. Can I come up to T's and stay with you for a week?"

It was Harry's use of the word "home" that impacted me so greatly, because I couldn't recall her using that word before. "*I'll see you in Boston*," sounded familiar enough, but "home"? No. I gave it some thought, and I don't think she thought of my house in Newton as home. Perhaps, in her mind, it was "*Faye's house*" or "*my sister's house*," but not hers. It made me want to cry, because I don't know that Harry's had a place to call home since my parents passed away.

And now, suddenly, she's referring to Fairbanks as home. I'm so touched by this development, because it has taught me something important too: "home" isn't really a set place like an apartment or a house. It's just whatever place on earth holds the people that love you. I love Harry, so her home is with me. And Trevor loves me, so my home is with him. And the Starlings love Trevor, so his home is with them.

And that's why I've decided to live in Fairbanks. Permanently. Trevor has invited me to stay indefinitely, and it's an invitation I mean to accept. In the strangest turn of events, one that I never saw coming, I use my freedom of choice to make Fairbanks, Alaska, my home.

Karl Franklin doesn't know it yet, but he's going to be offered the Boston CEO job on a permanent basis, and then he's going to help me find his counterpart for the Seattle office. I can happily be in Boston once or twice a month for important meetings, and I can easily be in Seattle once or twice a week for the same, but I cannot *live* bicoastally and still prioritize my relationship with Trevor. And Trevor ties with Harry for my first priority moving forward.

I read the note again, wondering where the driver is taking me tonight, then remembering that I have an appointment with my orthopedist at ten o'clock.

I'd better get in the shower if I want to be on time.

***

"Has anyone ever told you that you're a fast healer, Ms. Findley?"

"Not that I can recall," I tell the doctor, who's inspecting my foot.

Dr. Knotts nods at me. "Well, you are. This looks great."

"I've had some amazing support over the last six weeks. My boyfriend has been my own personal superhero," I tell him.

I think about the many times Trevor carried me up and down stairs, made meals for us, helped me shower, or brought me a cup of coffee. Cheerfully, with sweetness and love, he nursed me back to health. If I am a fast healer, it's not because of me. It's all because of Trevor.

"Good man."

"*I* certainly think so."

"You don't need the boot anymore," he tells me, making a note on my chart. "You need to move slowly and carefully over the next few months, but you can to start trusting your foot again."

"Okay. Sounds good." I pause, then ask, "Air travel?"

"I wouldn't recommend anything longer than a few hours, but yes, you can fly. Be warned, however, your foot will swell, and it could delay your healing process."

"So weekly flights—"

"Would be a stupid choice for a smart woman to make," he says, giving me a look. "Listen, I'm prescribing some physical therapy too, but I'm not certain you'll be staying in Fairbanks. Should I write it out generically? So you can share it with your physician in Boston?"

"No, actually," I say for the first time out loud. "I'll be staying in Fairbanks on a permanent basis moving forward. Please suggest a local rehab center."

There's a knock on the exam room door, and a nurse sticks her head in the room.

"Dr. Knotts?"

"Yes?"

"Mr. Nosaka is on the phone again. Do you two minutes?"

He looks at me, and I nod. "Go ahead. I can wait."

"Don't go anywhere. I'll be back in a second."

The door closes behind Dr. Knotts, and I say it again, this time in a whisper, like I'm practicing to say it to Trevor tonight.

"I've decided to sell my house in Boston. I want to live here with you. Permanently." *Hmm. No. Not quite right.* "I want to live here with you...*indefinitely.*" *Yes. Better. Use the same word he used.*

I bite my lower lip. *Am I being too presumptuous?*

I rethink the conversation we had. He said that my having a Seattle office would make it easier for me to "stay," and then he further clarified his position by saying he wanted us to "figure out a way to stay together."

Hmm. He didn't actually ask me to move in with him.

Am I assuming too much here?

Is it possible he's suggesting that I get a place in Fairbanks and we continue to move forward in our relationship in a more conventional fashion? Did he mean "stay" in his house or "stay" in Fairbanks?

"You're going to drive yourself crazy," I mutter. "The only way to know is to talk about it."

But he loves me, I tell myself. *Doesn't that elevate his invitation to the next level? To the level of cohabitation? Or not?*

"Damn it," I whisper, crossing my arms over my chest. *Do other women go through these types of conversations with themselves?* Because I don't like it very much at all.

There's a crisp knock at the exam room door, and Dr. Knotts reenters the small room. "Sorry about that."

"No worries," I tell him, narrowing my eyes. He's a

man. An older man, but still a man. And we have the added benefit of doctor-patient confidentiality. "Dr. Knotts, can I ask you a question?"

"Of course."

"If you told a woman with whom you were in a sexual relationship that you wanted to 'stay together indefinitely,' what would that mean?"

He blinks at me. I don't think he was expecting this. "I'm really more of a bone doctor—"

"Yes, I know. But I'd still like your opinion," I tell him. "Oh! And in this specific scenario, the man has told the woman, at least once a day for a month or so, that he is 'in love' with her or that he loves her. That might be an important detail for your decision-making."

"My decision-making?"

"About the meaning of '*stay together indefinitely*.'"

I look at him expectantly, but he stares back at me saying nothing. Are we in a standoff?

"Doctor? A little help, please?"

He clears his throat, his cheeks coloring a touch.

"Okay. Well...I think...if I was in an intimate relationship with a woman, and I loved her, the words 'stay together indefinitely' wouldn't need much further clarification."

"Ah," I say. "But they do. Does it mean he wants me to stay here in Fairbanks, but in my own dwelling? Or is it an invitation to cohabit? Or, perhaps, it's meant to say that I can still live bicoastally, but when we have sex it's only with each other? There's a real gamut to the meaning, as you can see."

He purses his lips together. "Ms. Findley, don't you think these questions would be better directed to…him?"

"Of course," I say. "But I'm not very experienced with men…perhaps a more, you know, *experienced* woman would have already understood his meaning."

Dr. Knotts grins at me. "I doubt it. Men and women have, historically, spoken different languages. Mars. Venus. You know."

Actually, I don't, but astronomy feels off-topic.

"So you can't shed any light…? On the…whole *stay indefinitely* thing?"

"If I can be frank," he says, "I think you might be focusing on the wrong part of the conversation."

"How so?"

"I've been married for thirty-seven years, Ms. Findley, and I still love my wife. I *love* her. And that means that I'd do anything for her. Whatever it takes to make her happy and keep her happy." He smiles at me. "If this man truly loves you—and from what you've told me, the way he cared for you during your convalescence, you have little reason to doubt it—perhaps the answer to what *stay indefinitely* means, actually depends more on your interpretation than his."

"You're saying that he wants what I want?"

"I'm saying that if I was the man in a similar scenario with my wife…yes. Whatever staying indefinitely meant to her—whatever she wanted from me—is what I would cheerfully offer her."

"I want to stay in Fairbanks. With him," I say. "I want

his home to be my home."

"Then I'm pretty sure," Dr. Knotts says, handing me a printed sheet with my instructions for physical therapy, "you just need to let him know."

***

Trevor

When I get to the Chalet Blanche at six o'clock, I'm relieved that the desk clerk isn't the same young woman who witnessed my fight with Faye at the end of December. An older gentleman checks me in, confirming that a bottle of Louis Roederer Cristal Brut champagne is already in the room, chilling in a silver ice bucket, and that two steak dinners will be delivered to our room at 8:30 p.m. Aside from a phone call to alert me when Faye arrives, I make it clear that I want no additional interruptions, for any reason, during our stay. After the desk clerk nods in agreement, I take my room key and head down the white corridor off the main lobby.

Modern and elegant, our room has light-colored hardwood floors and white walls, decorated with tastefully framed, abstract black-and-white photography. A picture window takes up one whole side of the room, giving an unobstructed view of the mountains, and I say a quick prayer for the northern lights to dazzle us tonight. The bed in the center of the room is king-sized and plush, covered with a fluffy white duvet, and the bottle of champagne sits, as promised, on a bureau that shares the same light-wood tone as the floor.

Beside the wine, there is a note from the hotel wishing

us a happy Valentine's Day, two champagne flutes, and a bud vase with a single red rose. Nice. I approve.

Opening my suitcase, I take out a dozen neatly packed votive holders and candles, placing them around the room. I had a local florist fill a gallon Ziploc bag full of red rose petals for me, and I scatter them on the floor and bed. Satisfied that the room is suitably romantic, I place a change of clothes and my overnight bag in a bureau drawer, then hide the suitcase in the closet.

Standing at the window, with a million stars overhead, I reflect on the ways my life has changed over the last eight weeks.

I was a bitter, angry man when Faye Findley walked into the Golden Buddha on Christmas Eve. So consumed by my brother's betrayal and my broken engagement, I couldn't see a future ahead. I had placed an ad for anonymous sex because the idea of ever loving another woman was so frightening to me.

And then I met Faye.

And she changed my whole world.

Her hope and wonder were the perfect ballast to my bitter weariness.

Her devotion to her business made my devotion to mine seem like a strength in my character, not a flaw.

Her gentle advice about reconnecting with her own sibling, about cherishing those family members you have in your life, made me rethink my relationships with Marlena and Cez. I can see now that Marlena and I were not well suited, and I'm *almost* in a place to forgive Cez, though true rebuilding will likely take some time.

But more than anything, I am *excited* about the future…

Reaching inside my pocket, I take out the small velvet ring box and flip it open to look at the engagement ring I purchased yesterday.

…and I am *over-the-moon* at the prospect of asking the woman I love to be my wife.

Do I have a bit of apprehension over this enormous decision? I do. I think every man does. But I love her, and she loves me. We are, neither of us, too young or too flighty to make such an important commitment. But mostly, I want for Faye to know that when I suggested we stay together, I meant forever. We can have a long engagement, if that's her preference, but if I am going to ask her to relocate her entire life to Fairbanks, I need for her to know that I am ready to bind my life to hers in every way that matters…that I want to spend every day from now until the end of our days…

Together.

***

I'm still staring out the window, practicing my proposal, when the room phone rings informing me that Faye's car has arrived and the door man is helping her up the stairs to the lobby. I hurry down the hall to greet her, stepping into the lobby just as she walks through the entrance doors.

"No boot!" I exclaim, checking out her gray sweater dress with approval, though I note the sexy knee-high boots she could wear back in December won't fit right now. She's replaced them with black, furry slippers and looks adorable.

"No boot," she says, with a grin. "I'm officially bootless

now."

Pulling her into my arms in the center of the lobby, I hold her tightly. "Did you figure out where we were meeting?"

"I had my suspicions," she says.

Her hair, which she wears down as often as up, is in a loose bun tonight, as it was the night of our first date, a few days after Christmas.

I back up to look at her face, lightly made up with lip gloss and mascara. "You're beautiful."

"You're biased."

"Nah. I thought you were beautiful on Christmas Eve at the Golden Buddha."

"I love you," she whispers, her eyes glistening with emotion as she grins up at me.

Her words make my blood heat and my heart sing. "I love you too."

"So…now that you've got me here, whatever will you do with me?" she asks.

"I did say one bed and zero clothes, right?"

"You did," she says, arching against me. It's one of her "tells." She's getting turned on.

"Well, I think we should head to our room and—"

"Trev?"

I didn't hear the front doors open, but I recognize the voice calling to me from them. I look up from Faye's face, over her shoulder, to find Cez and Marlena standing just inside the inn's French doors.

It's the first time I've seen my little brother in the flesh since that terrible night last June.

"Cez," I murmur.

He clears his throat, his face registering worry. "Are you...staying here?"

Faye steps out of my arms and turns to face my brother.

"We are," I say.

"Oh," he says, shuffling his feet. "We are too."

It's an awkward conversation, with our respective women standing beside us, one of them quite obviously pregnant.

Faye steps forward with her hand outstretched. "We haven't met yet. I'm Faye. Faye Findley."

Cez's eyes skim from mine to hers as he steps forward to meet her, taking her hand. "Cecil Starling. I've...met your sister. Harry."

"She mentioned meeting all of you," Faye says. "She loved your mother's wassail."

I watch this interaction, frozen in place, admiring Faye's composure but uncertain that I'm ready to engage with my brother.

Faye turns to Marlena. "Hello, Marlena. We met in the ER, I believe."

Marlena's cheeks flush, and I realize how young and unsubstantial she looks beside Faye's maturity and grace.

"Y-Yeah. Are you—how's your foot? Oh!" She looks down at Faye's slippers. "Your boot's off, huh?"

"Just today," says Faye. "It's better, thank you for asking."

She looks over her shoulder at me, and though she says nothing, I know she is letting me decide what happens next. She has handled any requisite civility and pleasantries. We can easily leave the lobby now…or I can step forward, stand beside her, and wish my brother and his fiancée well. It's the softness in my girlfriend's eyes, which reminds me of what she said about giving almost anything for one more day with her parents, that propels me forward. I hold her eyes until the front of my body touches her back, then look up at my brother and his fiancée.

"You look well, Marlena."

"Thank you."

Taking a deep breath, I slide my eyes to Cez.

"Trev," he says, his eyes instantly filling with tears. "I…I…just…"

Faye's hand reaches behind to capture mine, and I lace our fingers together.

"I forgive you, Cez," I tell him, nodding as I take a deep and ragged breath. "It'll take some time for me to trust you, but I forgive you, brother."

He makes a small, strangled sound that slips through his tightly closed lips, blinking his eyes like crazy as he nods at me. After taking a stuttered breath through his nose and sniffling, he clears his throat.

"Thank you," he whispers, clearing his throat again, while wiping away some runaway tears. "I promise…I promise never, ever to hurt you like that again."

Faye squeezes my hand gently.

I nod at Cez, feeling my own eyes start to burn. I'm

eager to get away from him before I embarrass myself in public.

"Well," says Faye in a warm tone. "We wish you both a happy Valentine's Day. Will you excuse us? Have a lovely stay."

"Yeah," chirps Marlena. "You too."

"Of course," says Cez, who's just starting to get himself under control. "Good night."

I nod at him once more, then I turn around, headed back to our room, my hand still safely entwined with hers.

"You did a good thing," she says softly as we head down the hallway, out of earshot of the lobby.

The next breath I take is deep and restorative. "I don't think I could've done it without you."

"You would have, eventually," she says. "You were angry with him, but you still love him."

She's right. I do. But honestly, I've spent enough time on Cez for tonight.

"Now," I suggest, "how about we get on to the business of celebrating our first Valentine's Day together?"

"Sounds divine."

She grins up at me as I slide the keycard into the door reader, preceding me into the room and gasping lightly over the rose petals. She turns around to smile at me. "How beautiful. Did you do this for me?"

"Mm-hm."

"You're setting the bar very high for future Valentine's Days," she informs me, glancing at the ice bucket. "Wow! Is that Louis Roederer?"

"It is." I nod, crossing the room to join her. I take the bottle out of the bucket, feeling a galvanizing, a gathering inside of me. Is this the moment? I think it might be.

Opening the bottle with a satisfying *pop*, I pour two glasses, handing one to her, and raising the other.

"To us," I say.

"To us," she says.

"Don't drink yet," I tell her as she raises the flute to her lips.

"Why?"

I place my flute on the bureau, pull the little box from my pocket, and drop down on one knee before her. She gasps sharply, placing her free hand over her heart as I open the box to reveal a two-carat princess-cut diamond engagement ring.

"Trevor!"

I reach for her wineglass and place it on the floor, then take her free hand and hold it in mine.

"Faye. Sweetheart. I love you so much."

"I...love you too," she sobs, smiling at me through tears.

"This may feel fast, but the reality is that I know the difference between asking the wrong woman to marry me and asking the right one," I tell her. "*You* are the right woman for me. *You* are the person I want to spend the rest of my life with. I know what I want, Faye Findley. It's *you*. It'll *always* be you."

Tears slide down her face as she murmurs my name. "Trevor..."

"Please be my wife," I whisper in a rush. "Marry me."

My sweet woman, whom I love more than my life, sits down on my knee, wraps her arms around my neck and looks me in the eyes.

"Yes," she whispers.

"Yes?"

"Yes!" she cries, leaning forward to kiss me as I pull the ring from its velvet pillow.

When she draws back, I take her arm from around my neck and place the ring on the fourth finger of her left hand. She admires it for a second, then slides her eyes to mine...and they are full of wonder, and gratitude, and love.

"Now I know what 'stay indefinitely' means," she says, reaching up to wipe away her tears.

"It means I will love you to the end of time," I promise her, my body finally relaxing from the emotion of my proposal but starting to get turned on by the woman sitting on my knee and the huge bed behind us. I stand up, take her beringed hand in mine, and lead her over to the bed.

She pulls her dress over her head, blushing from head to toe when she explains. "I decided to go *commando*."

A second later, I'm as naked as she.

I sit on the edge of the bed and draw her onto my lap, sliding into the wet heat of her body as she lowers herself onto my erection.

She moans softly beside my ear, and she feels so fucking good, I'm about to lose all semblance of concentration, when she murmurs: "Mr. Fairbanks had it all wrong."

"What do you mean," I ask in a gravelly whisper, "he had it all wrong?"

"In the"—she gasps as I thrust forward again—"ad. He said, 'Zero chance of love.'" She arches her back so that our chests are flush and her heart beats against mine. She cups my face in her hands, looking deeply into my eyes and says, "What he didn't know...at the time...was that we had a one hundred percent chance of *true* love."

And because she's right—so very, very right—I kiss her like I will every day for the rest of my life, and then I worship her body with mine until dawn.

EPILOGUE

Faye

Though my in-laws, Barb and Linus, ask us to spend our second Christmas Eve with them, Trevor and I make other plans. We tell his parents we'll see them, and the rest of the family, tomorrow at the farm for Christmas Day.

The rest of the family now includes Aurora, who is five months old, and doted on by her grandparents, parents, uncles, and aunts...and Harry, who spent her spring break and most of her summer vacation in Fairbanks with us and acted as my maid of honor at our August wedding.

She arrived yesterday and decided to stay at Starling Farms tonight, where she is very welcome and well loved. The Starlings have more or less adopted Harry as the daughter they never had, and Barb, especially, has taken Harry under her colorful wings.

Harry even invited Barb and Linus to join me and Trevor at Cornell parent's weekend in October, an invitation they accepted with pleasure. I love that Harry has a mother figure in her life now, in addition to a big sister who tries very hard to be there for her in any and every way she needs me. And, of course, there's her "best friend in the whole world," Baz, who adores her.

Poor Baz, who picked up Harry at the airport yesterday, follows her around with his eyes whenever they are in the same room together. He is utterly in love with her, though he seems to recognize that biding his time is wise, for now. She's twenty-one and finishing college in June, after which she'll attend business school at University of Washington in Foster.

At twenty-one, Harry still has a good deal of growing and learning to do, and at twenty-six, Baz would be wise to wait for her and not to push her to grow up too quickly.

Though I admire his patience, I do not envy it.

Then again, Trevor once told me that Baz moves at the speed of glacial ice when it comes to women…so maybe a long wait for Harry is exactly what he needs. Only time will tell.

"Faye!"

Brandy reaches over the bar and gives me a hug, and I squeeze her back as best I can. Though we don't make it down to the Golden Buddha very often, being here on Christmas Eve felt right.

"Is T coming?"

"He is! He'll be here any second."

"What can I get you? A martini?"

"Umm. No. Thanks. How about sparkling water in a lowball glass with a lime?"

"*Water?* Are you planning to take a bath or somethi—" Suddenly she gasps in realization, placing her hands over her mouth. "Wait a second! Are you…?"

I grin at her, putting a finger over my lips and saying

nothing. No one knows yet. Not Harry. Not the Starlings. Not Trevor. And frankly, I think he should be the first to hear it, directly from me.

Brandy holds up her hands in understanding, then pretends to zip her mouth shut. "Mum's the word! He won't hear a peep from me. Don't you worry."

"Thanks," I say, looking around the bar as she makes my drink. I feel a little nostalgic, remembering last year. "We met here."

"I remember," says Brandy. "You thought we were a couple, and T was a jerk to you."

"He was hurting," I remind her. "But I might have left without knowing his story if you hadn't invited me to dinner. You told me everything. You helped me see him. I owe you, Brandy."

"Bartenders and matchmakers have a lot in common, Faye," she tells me, putting a cocktail napkin on the bar and my drink on top of it. From all outward appearances, I could be drinking a gin and tonic.

"Maybe you were both that night. Bartender *and* matchmaker."

"Maybe I was," she says, winking at me before stepping to the end of the bar to take someone else's order.

I sip my drink for a moment before I hear a familiar voice close to my ear. "So what's the verdict?"

The first words he ever spoke to me.

I turn to look at him. "I'm sorry, sir, but I'm meeting my husband here in a little bit."

"Can I keep you company until he gets here?"

"I don't think it's a good idea," I say, trying not to smile.

"Jealous type?"

"Not jealous, per se, but I'm just not the sort of girl who cheats."

"I bet he loves that about you," says T, leaning forward to claim my lips with his. He cradles my cheeks between his warm hands, and when he draws back from me, he looks as drunk as he did the first time he kissed me. "In fact, I know he does."

"How was your day, Mr. Starling?" I ask him as he settles his body on the stool I reserved for him beside me.

"Excellent, Mrs. Starling. How was yours?"

"Tremendous. Big deal out of Seattle today. It's going to make us the biggest distributor of Asian beer on the West Coast."

"The acquisitions guy you hired is working out?"

"He's great," I say, thinking of all the new hires I made this year and how the lessons of delegation that I learned during my days with a broken foot have changed my life for the better.

"T!" says Brandy. "Merry Christmas!"

"Hey, there," says Trevor. "You gonna be here tomorrow?"

"Of course! You?"

"We said we'd spend the day with my folks," says Trevor, flicking a glance at me, "but how would you feel about ending the night here?"

"I'd love it," I tell him, remembering the smorgasbord

of offerings on Ping's Christmas table last year. "Two years in a row makes it a tradition!"

"Awesome," says Brandy. "What're you drinking? Hard cider? Vodka on the rocks?"

"My wife's taste in drinks is excellent." He grins. "I'll have whatever she's having."

Brandy blinks at him. "You want...what she's having?"

"Absolutely," he says, turning his body to face me. Before I can stop him, he picks up the glass and takes a big sip, then puts it back down on the bar slowly. "Is that...*seltzer*?"

"I'll give you two a minute," says Brandy, sliding away.

"It is," I say, trying desperately not to smile as I watch him trying to figure this out.

"Why in the world are you drinking water?"

I can't help myself. My smile comes bursting forth, and I just sit there, on a barstool at the Golden Buddha on Christmas Eve, smiling like it's the happiest day of my life...and in a year that's offered me one beautiful day after another, it just might be.

"Hmm," I tease. "Why would a newly married young woman, who has sex with her husband every night and ten times on the weekend, be drinking water instead of—"

His gasp is so loud, it cuts me off, and his mint-colored eyes are wider than I've ever seen them before. "Oh, my God! Faye! Sweetheart! Are you...are you...?"

"Pregnant?" I ask him, giggling as tears track down my face. "Yes!"

I'm in his arms a second later, and he's dragging me off

the barstool so he can kiss me. Finally, he leans away, looking at me with glistening eyes.

"You're carrying my baby."

"I am. Yes."

He pulls me close again and I can feel the fierce and thunderous beat of his heart.

Outside the snow is falling, and I definitely won't be drinking a scorpion bowl (*or two*) tonight, but everything I hoped for when I flew to Fairbanks that Christmas Eve last year has already come true.

Including the fact that Mr. Fairbanks, who gave himself a zero percent chance of love, now has enough to last him a lifetime.

THE END

ALSO BY KATY

a modern fairytale
(A collection)

The Vixen and the Vet
Never Let You Go
Ginger's Heart
Dark Sexy Knight
Don't Speak
Shear Heaven
Fragments of Ash

THE BLUEBERRY LANE SERIES

THE ENGLISH BROTHERS
(Blueberry Lane Books #1–7)

Breaking Up with Barrett
Falling for Fitz
Anyone but Alex
Seduced by Stratton
Wild about Weston
Kiss Me Kate
Marrying Mr. English

THE WINSLOW BROTHERS
(Blueberry Lane Books #8–11)

Bidding on Brooks
Proposing to Preston
Crazy about Cameron
Campaigning for Christopher

THE ROUSSEAUS
(Blueberry Lane Books #12–14)

Jonquils for Jax
Marry Me Mad
J.C. and the Bijoux Jolis

THE STORY SISTERS
(Blueberry Lane Books #15–17)

The Bohemian and the Businessman
The Director and Don Juan
Countdown to Midnight

THE SUMMERHAVEN SERIES

Fighting Irish
Smiling Irish
Loving Irish
Catching Irish

THE ARRANGED DUO

Arrange Me
Arrange Us

ODDS ARE GOOD SERIES

Single in Sitka
Nome-o Seeks Juliet
A Fairbanks Affair
My Valdez Valentine
Kodiak Lumberjack

STAND-ALONE BOOKS:

After We Break
(a stand-alone second-chance romance)

Frosted
(a stand-alone romance novella for mature readers)

Unloved, a love story
(a stand-alone suspenseful romance)

Under the sweet-romance pen name
Katy Paige

THE LINDSTROMS

Proxy Bride
Missy's Wish
Sweet Hearts
Choose Me
Virtually Mine
Unforgettable You
My Treasure – all new!
Summer's Winter – all new!

Under the paranormal pen name
K. P. Kelley

It's You, Book 1
It's You, Book 2

Under the YA pen name
Callie Henry

A Date for Hannah

ABOUT THE AUTHOR

New York Times and *USA Today* bestselling author Katy Regnery started her writing career by enrolling in a short story class in January 2012. One year later, she signed her first contract, and Katy's first novel was published in September 2013.

Over forty-five books and three RITA® nominations later, Katy claims authorship of the multititled Blueberry Lane series, the A Modern Fairytale collection, the Summerhaven series, the Arranged duo, and several other stand-alone romances, including the critically acclaimed mainstream fiction novel *Unloved, a love story*.

Katy's books are available in English, French, German, Hebrew, Italian, Polish, Portuguese, and Turkish.